Chloe King has

~~9 Lives~~

8

7

6

5

4

3

2

1

W9-BVH-503

the nine lives of chloe king

The Fallen

The Stolen
(coming soon)

the nine lives of chloe king

VOLUME ONE

The Fallen

by
CELIA THOMSON

SIMON PULSE
New York   London   Toronto   Sydney

For John Ordover and Dave Mack, good friends
and the sine qua nons of my career and marriage

First Simon Pulse edition June 2004

Copyright © 2004 by 17th Street Productions, an Alloy company

SIMON PULSE
An imprint of Simon & Schuster Children's Publishing Division
1230 Avenue of the Americas, New York, NY 10020

Produced by 17th Street Productions,
an Alloy company
151 West 26th Street
New York, NY 10001

Printed in the United States of America
10 9 8 7 6 5 4 3 2 1

Library of Congress Control Number 2004102854
ISBN: 0-689-86658-5

Prologue

He never tired or lost her trail.

Not since she'd first seen him an hour ago in the bar, when his sleeve had fallen back and revealed an ornate black brand. Scrolls and curlicues of ink and scar tissue spelled out the familiar words: *Sodalitas Gladii Decimi.*

And so she ran.

She took a deep breath and looked ahead, leaping over piles of garbage and puddles with the precision of an acrobat, propelled by her terror. Which street did this alley connect to? Was there a public place close by—even a twenty-four-hour gas station—where she would be safe?

Finally the smell of open, wet air told her an exit was ahead: a barbedwire-topped gate blocked the far end of the alley.

She prepared to leap, triumph and freedom singing in her ears.

Then something burned into her left leg, ripping through muscle.

She clung to the gate, her leg dangling uselessly below her. She reached to pull herself up, hand over hand, but a near-silent whir announced a second attack. In an instant, she fell.

"Trapped, I'm afraid," said an irritatingly calm voice.

She desperately tried to push herself along the ground, away from him—but there was nowhere to go.

"Please . . . no . . . ," she whimpered, pushing herself back up against a wall. "I'm not what you think. I'm not *bad.* . . ."

"I'm sure you don't believe you are."

She heard a blade, fine and small like a dagger, being whisked out of its sheath.

"I've never—I would never hurt *anyone*! Please!"

He cut her throat.

"Id tibi facio, Deus," he whispered, putting the side of his left hand to his heart, thumb in the middle of his chest, pointing up. A gentle sigh escaped the dying girl; a thin ribbon of blood trickled down her neck. Tiny marks of an expert assassin. He bowed his head. "In allegiance to the Order of the Tenth Blade. *Pater noster, rex gentius.*"

He adjusted her head so that she looked more comfortable and closed her eyes. Then he wiped the tiny silver blade on a handkerchief, sat back on his heels, and waited.

When she woke up, he would kill her again.

One

As soon as she opened her eyes that morning, Chloe decided that she would go to Coit Tower instead of Parker S. Shannon High, her usual destination on a Tuesday.

She was turning sixteen in less than twenty-four hours, with no real celebration in sight: Paul spent Wednesdays at his dad's house in Oakland, and—far worse—her mom had said something about "maybe going to a nice restaurant." What was a "nice" restaurant, anyway? A place where they served blowfish and foie gras? Where the wine list was thicker than her American civilization textbook? No, thank you.

If Mom found out about the Coit Tower expedition, Chloe would be grounded, completely eliminating any possibility of dinner out. Then Chloe would have a *right* to feel miserable on her sixteenth birthday, at home, alone, punished. The idea was strangely alluring.

She called Amy.

"Hey, want to go to the tower today instead of physics?"

"Absolutely." There was no hesitation, no pause—no grogginess, in fact. For all of Amy's rebel post-punk posturing, Chloe's best friend was a morning person. How did she deal with the 2 A.M. poetry readings? "I'll see you there at ten. I'll bring bagels if you bring the crack."

By "crack" Amy meant Café Eland's distinctive twenty-ounce coffee, which was brewed with caffeinated water.

"You're on."

"You want me to call Paul?"

That was strange. Amy never volunteered to do anything, much less help with group planning.

"Nah, let me guilt him into it."

"Your funeral. See ya."

She dragged herself out of bed, wrapping the comforter around her. Like almost everything in the room, it was from Ikea. Her mom's taste ran toward orange, turquoise, abstract kokopelli statuettes, and blocks of sandstone—none of which fit in a crappy middle-class San Francisco ranch. And since Pateena Vintage Clothing paid a whopping $5.50 an hour, Chloe's design budget was limited. Scandinavian blocks of color and furniture with unpronounceable names would have to do for now. *Anything* beat New Southwest.

She stood in front of the closet, wearing a short pair of boxers and a tank. Even if she still hadn't gotten her period, Chloe was finally developing a waist, as if her belly had been squeezed up to her breasts and down to her butt. Hot or not, it wasn't as though any of it really mattered: her mom grounded her if she so much as even *mentioned* a boy other than Paul.

She threw herself in front of the computer with a wide yawn and jiggled the mouse. Unless Paul was asleep or dead, he could pretty much be located at his computer 24/7. Bingo—his name popped up in bold on her buddy list.

Chloe: Ame and me are going to Coit Tower today. Wanna come?
Paul: [long pause]
Chloe: ?
Paul: You're not gonna guilt me into it 'cause I'm not gonna be around for your birthday, right?
Chloe: :)
Paul: *groan* ok I'll tell Wiggins I got a National Honor Society field trip or something.
Chloe: ILU, PAUL!!!
Paul: Yeahyeah. Cul8r.

Chloe grinned. Maybe her birthday wasn't going to suck after all.

She looked out the window—yup, fog. In a city of fog, Inner Sunset was the foggiest part of San Francisco. Amy loved it because it was all spooky and mysterious and reminded her of England (although she had never been there). But Chloe was depressed by the damp and cheerless mornings, evenings, and afternoons and liked to flee to higher, sunnier ground—like Coit Tower—at every opportunity.

She decided to play it safe and dressed as if for school, in jeans and a tee and a jean jacket from Pateena's that was authentic eighties. It even had a verse of a Styx song penned carefully in ballpoint on one of the sleeves. She emptied her messenger bag of her textbooks and hid them under her bed. Then she stumbled downstairs, trying to emulate her usual tired-grumpy-morning-Chloe routine.

"You're down early," her mother said suspiciously.

Uneager to pick a fight this morning, Chloe swallowed her sigh. *Every*thing she did out of the ordinary since she'd turned twelve was greeted with suspicion. The first time she'd gotten a short haircut—paid for with her *own* money, thank you very much—her mother had demanded to know if she was a lesbian.

"I'm meeting Ame at the Beanery first," Chloe responded as politely as she could, grabbing an orange out of the fridge.

"I don't want to sound old-fashioned, but—"

"It's gonna stunt my growth?"

"It's a gateway drug." Mrs. King put her hands on her hips. In black Donna Karan capris with a silk-and-wool scoop neck and her pixie haircut, Chloe's mom didn't look like a mom. She looked like someone out of a Chardonnay ad.

"You have *got* to be kidding me," Chloe couldn't keep herself from saying.

6

"There's an article in the *Week*." Her mother's gray eyes narrowed, her expertly lined lips pursed. "Coffee leads to cigarettes leads to cocaine and crystal methamphetamines."

"Crystal *meth*, Mom. It's crystal *meth*." Chloe kissed her on the cheek as she walked past her to the door.

"I'm talking to you about not smoking, just like the ads say to!"

"Message received!" Chloe called back, waving without turning around.

She walked down to Irving Street, then continued walking north to the southern side of Golden Gate Park, stopping at Café Eland for the two promised coffees. Paul didn't partake; she got him a diet Coke instead. Amy was already at the bus stop, juggling a bag of bagels, her army pack, and a cell phone.

"You know, real punks don't—" Chloe put her hand to her ear and shook it, mimicking a phone.

"Bite me." Amy put down her bag and threw her phone in, pretending not to care about it. Today she wore a short plaid kiltlike skirt, a black turtleneck, fishnets, and cat-eye glasses; the overall effect was somewhere between rebellious librarian and geek-punk.

The two of them were comfortably silent on the bus, just drinking coffee and glad to have a seat. Amy might be a morning person, but Chloe needed at least another hour before she would be truly sociable. Her best friend had learned that years ago and politely accommodated her.

There wasn't much to look at out the bus window; just another black-and-white-and-gray early morning in San Francisco, full of grumpy-faced people going to work and bums finding their street corners. Chloe's reflection in the dusty window was almost monochromatic except for her light hazel eyes. They glowed almost orange in the light when the bus got to Kearny Street and the sun broke through.

Chloe felt her spirits rise: this was the San Francisco of postcards and dreams, a city of ocean and sky and sun. It really was glorious.

Paul was already there, sitting on the steps of the tower, reading a comic book.

"Happy pre-birthday, Chlo," he said, getting up and lightly kissing her on the cheek, a surprisingly mature, touchy-feely act. He held out a brown bag.

Chloe smiled curiously and then opened it—a plastic bottle of Popov vodka was nestled within.

"Hey, I figure if we're going to be truants, why not go all the way?" He grinned, his eyes squeezing into slits zipped shut by his lashes. There was a slight indentation in his short, black, and overgelled hair where his earphones had rested.

"Thanks, Paul." She pointed up. "Shall we?"

"What if you had to choose just one of these views to look at for the rest of your life," Chloe said. "Which one would it be?"

Amy and Paul looked up from each other, almost intrigued. The three of them had been sitting around for the past hour, not really doing much, with Chloe's two best friends occasionally exchanging giggly glances. That had grown old real fast.

Half of Coit Tower's windows showed spectacular, sun-drenched San Francisco scenery, the other nine looked out into a formless, gray-white abyss.

"I'd wait until the sun cleared before making my choice," Amy said, pragmatic as ever. She swirled her cup of coffee for emphasis, mixing its contents. Chloe sighed; she should have expected that answer.

Paul walked from window to window, game. "Well, the bridge is beautiful, with all the fog and clouds and sunset and dawn—"

"Bor-ing," Amy cut in.

"The Transamerica Pyramid is too sharp and weird—"

"And *phallic*."

"I guess I would choose the harbor," Paul decided. Looking over his shoulder, Chloe could see colorful little sailboats coming and going with the wind, dreamy, hazy islands in the distance. She smiled. It was a *very* Paul choice.

"Definitely *not* Russian Hill," Amy added, trying to regain control of the conversation. "Fugly sprawl with a capital *Fug*."

"Made your decision just in time, Paul . . ."

As they watched, low clouds came rolling down from

the hills, replacing each of the nine windows, enclosing the views in a white, total darkness. What should have been a beautiful blue day with puffy white clouds, now that they were out of Inner Sunset, had rapidly given way to the same old stupid weather.

This wasn't exactly what Chloe had expected for her sixteenth-birthday-school-blow-off day.

To be fair, she always expected more than life was likely to give: in this case, a golden sunny *Stand by Me/Ferris Bueller* these-are-the-best-days-of-our-lives sort of experience.

"So dude," Amy said, changing the subject. "What's up with you and Comrade Ilychovich?"

Chloe sighed and sank down against the wall, taking a last swallow from her own cup. Like Amy's, it was spiked with Paul's birthday present to her. Paul had already drunk his diet Coke and was now sipping directly from the amazingly cheesy plastic vodka flask. Chloe looked dreamily at the black-and-red onion domes on the label.

"He's . . . just . . . so . . . *hot*."

"And *so* out of your league," Amy pointed out.

"Alyec is steely-eyed, chisel-faced young Russian," Paul said with a thick cold war accent. "Possibly with modeling contract. Sources say Agent Keira Hendelson getting close to his . . . *cover*."

"Screw her." Chloe threw her empty cup at the wall, picturing it smashing into the student council's blond little president.

"You *could* be related, you know," Amy pointed out. "That could be a problem. He could be a cousin or nephew or something of your biological parents."

"The old Soviet Union's a big place. Genetically, I think we're okay. It's the getting to actually *date* him that's the problem."

"You could just, I don't know, go up to him and like, *talk* to him or something," Paul suggested.

"He's always surrounded by the Blond One and her Gang of Four," Chloe reminded him.

"Nothing gained, nothing lost."

Yeah, right. Like *he* had ever asked anyone out.

Amy swigged the last of her coffee and belched. "Oh, crap, I've got to pee."

Paul blushed. He always got nervous when either Amy or Chloe discussed anything like bodily functions in front of him—so usually Chloe didn't talk about that stuff when he was around.

But today she felt . . . well, odd. Jumpy, impatient. Not to mention a little annoyed with both him *and* Amy. This was supposed to be *her* birthday thing. So far it sucked.

"Too bad you can't do it standing up, like Paul," she said, watching him blush out of the corner of her eye. "You could go over the edge."

Now, what had made her say that?

She stood up. Leaning against the stone wall, Chloe peered down. All she could see was swirling whiteness and, off to her left, one water-stained red pylon of the Golden Gate Bridge.

What would happen if I dropped a penny from up here? Chloe wondered. *Would it make a tunnel through the fog? That would be cool.* A tunnel two hundred feet long and half an inch across.

She climbed up into a window and dug into her jeans pocket, hunting for spare change, not bothering to put her other hand on the wall for balance.

The tower suddenly seemed to tilt forward.

"What—," she began to say.

Chloe tried to resteady herself by leaning back into the window frame, grasping for the wall, but the fog had left it clammy and slick. She pitched forward, her left foot slipping out from beneath her.

"Chloe!"

She threw her arms back, desperately trying to rebalance herself. For a brief second she felt Paul's warm fingers against her own. She looked into his face—a smile of relief broke across it, pink flushed across the tops of his high cheekbones. But then the moment was over: Amy was shrieking and Chloe felt nothing catch her as she slipped out of Paul's grasp. She was falling—*falling*—out of the window and off the tower.

This is not happening, Chloe thought. *This is not the way I end.*

She heard the already-muffled screams of her friends

getting fainter, farther and farther away. Something would save her, right?

Her head hit last.

The pain was unbearable, bone crushing and nauseating—the sharp shards of a hundred needles being forced through her as her body compacted itself on the ground.

Everything went black, and Chloe waited to die.

Two

She was surrounded by darkness.

Strange noises, padding footsteps, and the occasional scream echoed and died in strange ways, like she was in a vast cavern riddled with tunnels and caves. Somewhere ahead and far below her, like she was standing at the edge of a cliff, was an indistinct halo of hazy light. It rippled unpleasantly. She started to back away from it. Then something growled behind her and shoved her hard.

Chloe pitched forward toward the light and into empty space.

This was it. This was *death*.

"Chloe? *Chloe?*"

That was odd. God sounded kind of annoying. Kind of whiny.

"Oh my God, she's—"

"Call 911!"

"There's no way she could have survived that fall—"

"GET OUT OF MY WAY!"

Chloe felt like she was spinning, her weight being forced back into her skin.

"You *stupid shithead*!"

That was Amy. That was *definitely* Amy.

"We should call her mom. . . ."

"What do we say? That Chloe is . . . that Chloe's *dead*?"

"Don't say that! It's not true!"

Chloe opened her eyes.

"Oh my God—Chloe . . . ?"

Paul and Amy were leaning over her. Tears and streaky lightning bolts of black makeup ran down Amy's cheeks, and her light blue eyes were wide and rimmed with red.

"You're a-alive?" Paul asked, face white with awe. "There's no way you could have—" He put a hand behind her head, feeling her neck and skull. When he pulled it back, there was only a little blood on his finger.

"You—you didn't—oh my God, it's . . . a . . . miracle . . . ," Amy said slowly.

"Can you move?" Paul asked quietly.

Chloe sat up. It was the hardest thing she could ever remember doing, like pushing herself through a million pounds of dirt. Her head swam, and for a moment there was two of everything, four flat gingerbread friends in front of her. She coughed, then began puking. She tried to lean to the side but couldn't control her body.

After she finished heaving, Chloe noticed that Paul

and Amy were touching her, holding her shoulders. She could just barely feel their hands; sensation slowly crept back over her skin.

"You *should* be dead," said Paul. "There is no. Way. You could have survived that fall."

She was struck by what he said; it seemed true. Yet here she was, alive. Just like that. Why was she so unsurprised?

"Help me up," Chloe said, trying not to notice the confused and frightened looks on her friends' faces. They helped Chloe lean forward, then slowly rise on shaky legs. She pointed her toes and bent her knees. They worked. Barely.

"Holy shit," said Paul, unable to think of anything else to say.

"We should get you to a hospital," Amy suggested.

"No," Chloe answered, faster than she meant.

"Are you *insane*?" Paul demanded. "Just because you're not dead doesn't mean you don't have a concussion or something. . . . You can't just fall two hundred feet and walk away without *some*thing happening."

Chloe didn't like the way her friends were looking at her. Shouldn't they be overjoyed? Thrilled that she wasn't dead? Instead they were looking at her like she was a ghost. "Yeah. We're going. No arguments," Amy said, stubbornly setting her pointy chin.

She and Paul helped Chloe up, one at each shoulder. *My devil and my angel*, Chloe thought ironically. *Well, my nerd and my wanna-be outsider.* Her head pounded, and she wanted nothing more than some aspirin.

And time alone to *think*.

She managed to get time to think in the emergency room, though she wasn't exactly alone. After Amy made a big hysterical deal about her *friend* and the *accident* she'd had, the reception nurse took one look at the healthy-seeming girl and relegated the three of them to the waiting room, behind a line of homeless people with visible damage: broken arms, scraped-up faces, oozing sores.

Paul took over filling out the contact information and paperwork, but after an hour of playing Guess the Symptom in her head, Chloe finally lost it.

"Look, why don't we just get out of here," she hissed. "I'm *fine*."

"As if," Paul said, reaching for a three-month-old *Vogue*.

"Don't touch that," Amy said, smacking his hand down. "Germs." Then she turned to Chloe. "You fell like a million feet onto your *head*, Chlo."

Another half hour passed. They watched the muted news flitting by incomprehensibly overhead, stories about Iraq and Wall Street and some girl's body found in an alley.

Finally, at four o'clock, the staff was ready to let in the girl with no visible injuries. The reception nurse put up her hand when Amy and Paul tried to follow.

"Only family," she said.

Amy turned to Chloe, wrinkling her freckled nose and smiling. It was a "cute" look that Chloe knew she had practiced in front of the mirror for hours, but it just didn't work with her friend's regal nose. "You'll be okay, I promise."

I know. I am okay.

"Thanks. For everything." Chloe gave her a lopsided smile, then went through the big, double-swinging metal door.

"If you and your friends are lying about your 'accident,'" she heard the nurse saying to Amy and Paul, "her parents are going to owe their insurance company a *whopper. . . .*"

As soon as the door swung shut behind her, Chloe scanned the hall for the exit.

She wished she had money for a cab, but she had to take the bus instead. As soon as she was inside her house, Chloe ran into the bathroom, tore off her clothes, and turned on the water. After a long soak she finally began to feel normal again, as if a few minutes of downtime by herself were all she really needed. *To recover from a two-hundred-foot fall.* She wrapped the towel around herself when she got out and looked in the mirror. There was a slight bruise on her temple and some dried blood on her scalp that was kind of fun to pick at. That was all.

Chloe wandered out and sat in front of her computer,

where her day had begun just a few strange hours before. She called up Google and then paused, her normally super-speed fingers hesitating over the keyboard. *How do you research "chances of surviving a crazy long fall onto pavement"?* A few minutes of surfing unearthed the interesting but useless fact that *defenestration* meant "the act of pushing someone out a window" and that almost no one besides Jackie Chan had easily survived a fall of much more than fifty feet.

Chloe got into bed and contemplated the ceiling. There was no way around it: she should not have survived her plummet from Coit Tower. Maybe this was the afterlife, and she was being eased into it slowly with familiar people and places?

She dismissed that quickly, though, picking some more blood out of her hair. *Heaven would be cleaner,* she thought decisively. But something strange had definitely happened. She should not be alive.

It was really a miracle.

Thinking in the autumnal afternoon light, Chloe drifted off to sleep.

She dreamed:

She lay in a comfortable hollow that was soft but did not move the way a mattress should when she shifted position. It was hot but not unpleasant; the sun's rays were tangible on her skin, caressing her back into sleep. Something licked the side of her face, rough and quick: *Get up.*

Chloe rose from the sand, dusted herself off. She shielded her eyes and looked to the horizon. This was no beach: it was a desert, empty and vast—but familiar and not frightening. The dunes were golden and the sky a dark empty blue, foreshadowing a chilly night when the sun finally set, half a day from now. They were heading to the north, down the river.

Below her hand was the lion that had woken her; it nuzzled at her fingers. They were all lions around her, female and maneless, the real power of the pride. Four of them. She was upright and awkward; when they finally started moving, the great cats had to slow their normal pace so she could keep up. Their beautiful shoulders rose and fell in a languid, powerful rhythm.

A vulture circled in the sky, hoping to feast on whatever they left.

When Chloe woke up, she was ravenous.

In the first moment of wakefulness after opening her eyes, before remembering her fall or being brought home, Chloe thought about what might be in the fridge. The rest came back to her as she got up. She was stiff, but even the bruise on her forehead was already fading.

She was surprised to see that the clock on the microwave read six; she had napped for over four hours. *Doesn't feel like it.* She opened the fridge and surveyed its contents, most of which were ingredients for whatever complicated gourmet dinner her mother was planning next. She pulled out a couple of yogurts, a pint of macaroni salad, and an old carton of lo mein. If falling two hundred feet didn't kill her, this probably wouldn't, either.

Chloe sat at the table and ate, still not fully awake, still not fully thinking, just enjoying the feeling of the food hitting her stomach and filling it.

The door slammed open and Mrs. King threw herself in. She opened her mouth to say something, then noticed the demolished feast on their table.

"I fell off Coit Tower today," Chloe said without thinking.

She hadn't planned on telling her mother immediately. She'd wanted to think it over first, plan the right approach—but she hadn't come up with one. Apparently her subconscious had.

"I know," her mother said in a low, angry tone. "I just came from the *hospital*, where you were supposed to be waiting for me. But no, you decided not to stay there, just like you *apparently* decided not to go to school today."

Daughter and mother looked into each other's eyes, not saying anything for a moment.

"*What* has gotten into you?" Chloe's mother finally yelled. "Is this the week you decided to get all of your teenage rebelling out at once?"

"Mom!" Chloe shouted back. "I *fell off Coit Tower*. Doesn't that mean anything to you?"

"Besides the fact that you were acting like an irresponsible idiot?"

But Mrs. King's eyes flitted to the light marks on her daughter's face, the uncomfortable way she was sitting, the black blood on her scalp.

"Are you okay?" she finally asked.

Chloe shrugged.

"That's why I left," she mumbled. "There wasn't anything wrong. They wouldn't listen to me."

"I'm glad Amy and Paul had the good sense to ignore you and bring you in." Mrs. King sighed. "Though I could kill them for encouraging your 'day off.'"

"Paul wasn't going to be around for my birthday," Chloe said, feeling like an idiotic, self-pitying brat as she said it. "I wanted to celebrate it with my friends."

Her mother opened her mouth to say something about that, but closed it again.

"You could have been killed," she said. She was quiet for a moment. "It's a miracle you weren't."

"I know."

There was another moment of silence. Chloe stared at her empty plate, and her mother stared at her. Mrs. King readjusted her black-rimmed glasses. Chloe could almost see her mom's thoughts tumbling around in logical lawyer circles: *She should be dead. She's not. I should be grateful. I'm angry with her. She's not dead. Therefore she must be punished.*

"We're going to have to talk about this. About your behavior and your punishment."

"*Obviously,*" Chloe said with heavy irony, suddenly irked. "Mom, I should be *dead.*"

"So? You're not. Be grateful. I have some steaks. . . .
I'll make them in an hour, after I do some paperwork."

"Did you *hear* me? I could—I *should* have been killed!!!"

Her mother opened her mouth to say something but
didn't. She ran her fingers through the wispy bangs that
framed her face, pushing it out of her eyes. Her hair was
thick and blond, as far from the color and texture of
Chloe's own hair as it was possible to get.

Chloe turned and stomped up to her room.

Maybe *she* was the one on drugs.

It was the only explanation Chloe could think of to
explain such a blasé reaction. Maybe it was shock?
Maybe she really didn't care. Chloe bitterly considered
how easily her mom could have been rid of her. She
would be free to throw dinner parties, go to gallery
openings, and maybe pick up a really cool boyfriend.
The kind who stayed away from complicated situations
like *daughters*. Especially adopted ones.

She thought about the father she could barely
remember, gone when she was four. *He* would have
cared. He would have rushed her *back* to the hospital,
no matter how much she protested.

Chloe sat on her bed and carefully opened the middle drawer of her bureau. It was the only old piece of
furniture in the room, ancient, solid, and oak. Perfect
for hiding the only real secret from her mom.

A little gray mouse sat up on his hind legs and
looked up at her expectantly.

Squeak!

Chloe smiled and put her hand down next to him, letting the mouse run up it. Her mother absolutely forbade all furred pets—supposedly because of her allergies. But back when her mom had gone on a rampant extermination phase, convinced that the house was overrun with vermin from their less cleanly neighbors next door, Chloe had come home from school one day and found the baby gray mouse in a live trap. With Amy and Paul's help she'd installed a light in her bureau. Now Mus-mus had a water dropper, a feeder, and an exercise wheel. This was a whole little world her mother knew nothing about.

She took a Cheerio out of the sandwich bag she kept under her bed and carefully held it out to him; the little mouse grabbed it with its front paws and sat back, nibbling as if it was a giant bagel.

"What should I do?" she whispered. The little mouse never stopped eating, ignoring her. "My mom is such a bitch."

Calling Amy was the only thing to do, really Chloe could apologize for acting so weird after she and Paul had taken her to the hospital, thank her for it, then get into the nitty-gritty of how bizarre it was to be alive and discuss why she had survived. Amy would probably offer some explanation involving the supernatural or angels—useless but entertaining. Chloe smiled and picked up the phone, dropping Mus-mus carefully back into his cage.

Seven long rings . . . Amy's cell phone was on, but she wasn't picking up. Chloe tried three more times in case the phone was buried at the bottom of Amy's bag and she couldn't hear it. On the fourth try Chloe left a message.

"Hey, Ame, call me. I'm—uh—feeling better. Sorry about the total rudeness today. I guess I was in shock or something."

She tried her at home.

"Oh, hello, Chlo-ee!" Mrs. Scotkin answered. There was a pause; she must have looked at a clock. "Happy sixteenth birthday in six hours!"

Chloe smiled despite herself. Amy must not have told her anything. "Thanks, Mrs. Scotkin. Is Amy around?"

"No—I think she's working on the Am civ project with her group tonight. Try her cell."

I did, thanks. "Okay, I will. Thanks, Mrs. Scotkin."

Chloe frowned. She went to the computer and checked all of Amy's aliases, but none of them were on. Maybe she really was doing homework? Nah. Paul was on but afk—Chloe didn't really feel like talking to him anyway. She needed *Amy*. She had almost died. It would be her birthday in four hours. Her mom was crazy. And she was All Alone.

She wandered around her room, picking up little things—pieces of bric-a-brac, stuffed animals—and putting them back down again. Her gloom gave way to restlessness; the room suddenly seemed very small. Too small for good brooding. She moved up and down on her toes like a ballerina.

Chloe stood for a moment, indecisive, then grabbed her jacket and banged down the stairs.

"Where are you going?" her mother demanded, like someone on a TV show.

"Out," Chloe responded, just as predictably. She even slammed the door behind her, just for good measure.

Chloe King has

~~9 Lives~~

8

7

6

5

4

3

2

1

Three

The night was chillier than Chloe expected. She stood for a moment in just her T-shirt, letting the moist air brush against her skin and lift the hair on her arms. It smelled surprisingly good; clean and wet as a cloud. Then the wind changed direction and she could hear and smell traffic at the same time: exhaust, acrid and dry even in the dampness, bit at her nose. Chloe sighed and put on her jacket.

Okay, Spontaneous One. Where to now?

She had set herself up for a *really* spectacular punishment later (though she hoped her near-death experience might help cut her some slack), so the night was not to be wasted. Then it came to her: *The Bank.*

Normally she would never, *ever* consider trying to get into the club without spending several hours dressing and redressing with Amy, going through everything in both their closets and sometimes even Paul's. Jeans and a tee were just embarrassing.

Chloe didn't care; she was going to do it. She was going to get into the club, by herself, dressed like the Creature from the Gap Lagoon. She just *needed* to dance right now.

It was a Tuesday, so there wasn't much of a line outside the club; its Christmas-from-hell orange and black fairy lights barely illuminated the otherwise empty street. One bored bouncer half sat on his stool, wearing tiny round black sunglasses that didn't reflect anything.

Chloe swaggered up to the velvet rope, unsure of what she was going to do. Everyone else in line was dressed in something sparkly, revealing, or all black—and was at least half a decade older.

Before she could think about it, Chloe sashayed past them and was asking the bouncer directly: "Hey, can I get in?" Just like that.

The giant man looked up at her and down, pausing at her scuffed black Converses. He cracked the barest hint of a smile. "I like your shoes. Those are *old* school, baby," he said, and unhooked the rope for Chloe.

"Thanks, man," she said in what she hoped was an equally cool voice. It was just like she'd passed a level in one of Paul's video games. Charon of Inner Sunset had just let her into the Dancing Afterworld.

The floor wasn't large, but it was surrounded by black mirrors that made it look twice as big and crowded. Clinging to the far wall and snaking around to the door was the enormous bar for which the place was famous: its surface was covered in thousands and thousands of shiny

30

copper pennies, shellacked into permanently flowing streams that ran all the way from a vault in the wall down to the floor.

During the day, when people vacuumed and cleaned and tried to remove the eternally beery stench, normal lights probably illuminated unpleasant details on the copper river—inky blots where people declared their fleeting love with Sharpies, worn and chipped places where coins had been hacked out, a night's work for the prize of a single penny. But for now it gleamed like an ancient god of wealth had just overturned his big pot of money. Bright, harsh golden lights bounced over it without shining on the patrons surrounding the bar, keeping their faces romantic and half lit.

The music was typical house with just a touch of electronica. No Moby *or* Goa here. Paul would have threatened to walk out, ears covered, before sidling up to the DJ to check out his equipment. It *should* have been the three of them there, not just her alone. But the music throbbed loudly, and Chloe felt like she could go out and dance by herself—she had almost died today; she could do anything.

She went to the bar first, leaning against it and surveying the scene. A few people were dancing and dressed badly, but otherwise it was a pretty hot crowd. What looked like an entire fraternity was loudly but good-naturedly arguing about sports, waving their beers, making an out-of-place businessman and his model very uncomfortable. There was one particularly hot guy across the floor, hanging around in the back, drinking quietly and people watching, just like her. He had black hair, dark skin, and light, light eyes. Exotic. She ducked her head to follow his movements as he ordered a beer, talked to a friend, and wandered into the crowd, but soon she lost him.

She waited patiently, but he didn't return. No one took his place, either; there were a few runners-up, but the hottest guy in the club had disappeared.

"Buy you a drink?"

He appeared at her side, smiling at her surprise and embarrassment. Up close he was even better looking, with full lips and a light spattering of darker brown freckles across his nose.

Chloe was just about to say No, thank you, like she did every time some twenty-something tried to pick up her fifteen-year-old self. But, "Absolutely!" was what came out instead.

"What'll it be?"

"Red Bull and vodka."

He nodded his approval and clinked her drink with his beer glass when the bartender handed it over.

"It's my birthday in two hours!" she shouted into his ear.

"Really? Cheers!" He sounded British. They toasted each other again and drank. "Happy birthday!" He kissed her delicately on her cheek. Chloe felt her stomach roll over and her mind play dead. An enormous grin spread over her face, completely destroying her cool. She had gotten into the club with no hassle, a drop-dead gorgeous guy just bought her a drink—this was turning out to be a pretty great birthday after all.

After another drink they started dancing. He moved in small sways and tiny circles perfect for avoiding other dancers in the tightly packed space. For one song he just put his hands around her waist and let her move, the center of his attention. When they walked through the crowd for a drink or a break, he would very lightly touch his hand to her back or shoulder, leading her protectively but not possessively.

"I'm Chloe!" she shouted at one point.

"I'm Xavier!" he shouted back.

At twelve thirty Chloe decided she was turning into a pumpkin. Near-death experience or no, her mother was going to kill Chloe *herself* if she stayed out all night. Xavier walked her out.

"Let me be the first to wish you a happy birthday," he said, kissing her gently on the lips in the dark parking lot. His mouth was warm and moist but not wet, and he was a hell of a lot more delicate than the few guys her own age Chloe had kissed. He pulled a card out of his wallet. It was actually engraved: *Xavier Akouri, 453 Mason St., #5A, 011-30-210-567-3981*. It took her a moment to realize that it was an international cell phone number she was looking at.

"Aren't you going to ask for mine?" Chloe asked.

He smiled and lowered his head so their noses were almost touching, looking directly into her eyes. "And would you have given me your real number? *You* call *me* if you want."

Her stomach did another flip-flop. Before she knew what she was doing, Chloe grabbed him around the back of the neck and held his head still while she kissed him. He actually let out a little moan. It drove her wild. His hands came up around her hips. Chloe reached around up and under his shirt to feel the skin on his back, kneading his muscles and clawing him with her fingernails. He moaned again, from pleasure or pain, it was hard to tell. But he took one of her legs and wrapped it up around his waist. Chloe felt herself sliding in closer and closer—

What the hell am I doing?

She opened her eyes and saw a handsome Euro kissing her, which might have been fine, wonderful, even—but she was inches from having sex with him in the middle of the parking lot.

"I'm sorry." She disentangled herself from him and backed off, breathing heavily. She ached and throbbed with want.

Xavier looked confused. His eyes were heavy lidded, and little beads of sweat held on like silver around his brow. His hair was tousled.

"I—I can't do this right now," she said.

To his credit, Xavier nodded, albeit reluctantly. "Do you—do you want to come back to my place?"

Chloe opened her mouth to say something. She realized it was very close to, Yes, I do—but managed to choke out, "I'm sorry," again, quickly turning and walking away. She ran all the way home and then once around the block for good measure, hoping to work the desire out of her body. Would her mom notice a look in her eye, a flush on her cheek? She could say it was from running.

When Chloe came in, her mother was reading on the couch, shoes off, glass of red wine on the table near her. Untouched. She was trying to make it look like she was just staying up late, not staying up for Chloe. Their eyes met.

"I'll be up in a little while," Mrs. King finally said. "I just want to finish this chapter."

She's actually going to be cool about this. Chloe couldn't believe it. And from her tone, it was like the late night out hadn't even happened—like maybe it would never be brought up again.

"Okay. G'night," Chloe said as gratefully as she could.

She staggered upstairs tiredly, taking her clothes off as she went. She could smell parts of Xavier on her shirt, his hands dangerously close to her breasts when they rested on her waist, his lips on her collar when he was kissing her neck.

She put on boxers and her oversized Invader Zim

T-shirt and fell into bed, holding her stuffed pig, still wondering what had happened. Teenage hormones, as they always said, or had it been an up-with-life reaction to her near-death experience? She thought she had heard of such a thing. . . . She clutched Wilbur more tightly and fell asleep.

Four

It was several hours into the next day, during first-period American civilization, when it suddenly hit Chloe: what she had done—or almost done—the night before, never mind the part about not dying. She had forgotten it all for a short, happy while.

This wasn't surprising; her brain barely began working before nine. The hours between being woken by her crappy old clock radio and second bell usually passed in a painless, mindless blur. Her mother, once upon a time playing the happy single mom, used to make her pancakes with syrup smiley faces and ask her about what she was doing that day. Eventually she gave up trying to communicate with her just-awake, mumbling daughter, filling the coffeemaker and setting the timer the night before instead. Chloe always tried to remember to grumble "bye" on her way out as Mrs. King did her morning yoga in front of the TV.

Holy crap. I almost had sex with a stranger in a parking lot last night.

Chloe felt tingles when she thought of Xavier; she could remember wanting him that badly but not the feeling itself. She idly tried to sketch his lips in the margin of her notebook. Where had she put his card?

". . . the same boot, for either foot. I don't think any of you kids today with your Florsheims or your tennis shoes could possibly imagine the suffering those soldiers marched in. . . ."

Neither Paul nor Amy was in this class, so it was triply boring. *What the heck is a Florsheim?* Chloe tried to cover a yawn, but it was so huge that it felt like her jaw had opened up wider than it was supposed to, like in *Alien.* Her teeth snapped back together when it was done, way too loudly. She looked around to see if anyone had noticed—no one except for Alyec, who was watching with raised eyebrows. She blushed but grinned back, actually looking him in his beautiful ice blue eyes. He smiled and made a "sleepy" gesture with his hands on the side of his face. Chloe nodded, and they each went back to note taking or doodling before Ms. Barker took notice.

When the bell rang, Chloe gathered her stuff and prepared to go to the library—it was such a bitch: she had *second* period free. Last year Amy had had first period free and often slept till eight before bothering to come in. As Chloe passed by the popular lockers, she

38

saw Alyec and waved. He was, of course, surrounded by the beautiful people.

Chloe thought about their little interaction in class and her success with the bouncer the night before and walked right up to him, ignoring the others.

"Didn't Am civ *suck* today?" Once again there she was, doing something she could not believe. First there was falling off a tower, then making out with a stranger, and now going directly up to the most-wanted guy in the junior class and talking to him. She could feel the vicious glares of his coterie impaling her backside, but somehow she wasn't the least bit nervous. Not even a heartbeat.

This is great. I should almost die every *day.*

"Oh, man," Alyec said in an accent that was fading but still had foreign overtones. "Watching you—how do you say—moan? Yes? That was the most exciting part of the hour."

"I wasn't moaning, I was *yawning*," Chloe said with a shy smile. "But if you find a way to make me moan, I'll let you watch all day." *Did I just say that?* She could see a whole bunch of jaws drop in her peripheral vision.

"You're hilarious, King, you know that?" He said it with a genuine laugh.

The second bell rang. "I've got to get to the library—but we should hang sometime."

Keira looked like she was actually going to growl; her lips were pulled back over her teeth.

"Absolutely," Alyec agreed. "Catch you later, King."

"See ya." She strolled past the other girls, trying not to look too smug but unable to keep from smiling a little.

Chloe thought about Xavier for most of her time in the library, staring out the windows and dreaming a little. She did the same during math and lunch. She thought about him more than her fall. It was kind of like her mom said—she fell, she survived, here she was. She was staring into space, pizza halfway to her mouth, when a familiarly annoying clap on her shoulder jolted her back to reality. Gobbets of bright orange oil flew across the table.

"Oh my God, is it *true*?" Amy threw herself into a seat next to her. "I mean, *happy birthday*, but ohmygod, is it really *true*, did you really flirt with Alyec right in front of Halley and Keira and—and everyone?"

"Yeah, I guess I did," Chloe said with a smile.

"How are you feeling?"

Chloe shrugged. "Fine, I think. A little weird. Last night—"

"Look, we gotta talk," Amy interrupted, leaning in close and looking her right in the eyes. "Something *big* is going down with me. I want to discuss. Dinner?"

Bigger than a near-death and near-sex experience? But Chloe bit back a sarcastic response; Amy really did look worried. And more intense than usual.

"Okay—"

"Cool! See you in English!"

Chloe watched her friend leap up and run off, safety pins and chains jangling as she went, unkempt chestnut hair bouncing. She turned back to her pizza and wondered when life would get back to normal. The grease had congealed into little solid pools of something like orange plastic. Chloe sighed and pushed it away.

Normality seemed to reassert itself at Pateena. As much as she hated sorting the clothes when they came back from the cleaner, there was a soothing familiarity in the folding and the straightening, the random tirades of the manager, the trendy customers. Nothing sexy *or* supernatural. Just a lot of jeans and overpriced old basketball shoes.

Chloe couldn't help noticing one customer who came in, though—just when she thought she had finally beaten her hormones down. He wore black cords, a ribbed black tee, and a black leather jacket, straight cut, like a regular suit jacket. But there were no hints of the über-goth about him: no tattoos or jewelry or fangs or anything. The outfit, which would have made anyone else look like a wanna-be Johnny Cash, worked perfectly on him; he had very dark brown hair, very slightly tanned, healthy skin, and deep brown eyes with beautiful long lashes.

The kicker, though, was his handmade black knitted cap with kitty cat ears.

Here was a handsome guy with a sense of humor. He thumbed through the polo shirts, frowning.

"Looking for a Halloween costume?" Lania asked him nastily. Chloe groaned, still unable to believe that the little alterna-bitch was allowed to operate the cash register and *she* wasn't. Just because the other girl was two years older. If Chloe had a dollar for every customer Lania insulted, she would finally be able to afford a new mountain bike. A *nice* one.

But he just chuckled. "No, I'm afraid it's for an actual meeting with actual executive types." He looked pretty young to be in business, but this was San Francisco, after all. He was probably a programmer or graphics designer or something.

Chloe went back to her work, wondering what Xavier looked like in the daylight. How many drinks did she have? Just two or three. She *could* have been beer goggling. Maybe those sexy freckles were actually bad acne. . . .

"Excuse me." The guy in the kitty hat carefully stepped around her, his purchases clutched to his chest. Apparently Lania had decided to let him pay.

"I like your hat," Chloe said.

"Really? Thanks!" He took it off and looked at it, as if he was surprised she'd noticed.

"Did your girlfriend make it?"

He grinned. "No, I did."

Chloe couldn't help being impressed. Besides Amy, almost no one she knew—not counting her mother's

42

trend-happy friends—knitted, and those who did never really finished anything. Except for some of the stitching, it looked pretty professional.

"I found the pattern on the Web," he continued. "If you knit, I'll give you the URL."

"No thanks, I can't. My friend Amy can, but I'm a complete spaz with my hands."

"Oh, you should totally take it up. It's kind of fun," he said, only a little embarrassed.

Chloe steeled herself for the usual touchy-feely sensitive guy discourse that was sure to follow, about how the movements were soothing, about how he felt in touch with people from long ago, about how some native culture or other did something spiritual with knitting needles, how he might want to open a shop someday, how it was good for teaching underprivileged kids self-esteem. . . .

But he had already turned to go.

"Well, see you," he said with a cute little half smile as he reached for the door. His eyes crinkled the upper part of his cheek, the skin pulled taut by a sexy scar that ran from the outside of his eye to just below his cheekbone.

Chloe waved and watched him go. Part of her was a little insulted; was she not a hot young girl who had attracted the notice of two hot guys in the last twenty-four hours? And Mr. Kitty Cat Man didn't even care. It was her *birthday*, for Christ's sake. Before her imminent grounding, didn't fate owe her something?

Then her butt vibrated.

She had to carefully dig her phone out of the back pocket of her own vintage jeans, which were men's and had a pre-worn white rectangle in the back where someone had once carried his wallet. Once in, her phone fit fine. Getting it out when she was any position but vertical was almost impossible.

Text message: *carluccis @ 7—a.*

Carlucci's was the place she and Amy had first met when the Scotkins had moved into the neighborhood. Maybe she'd get some decent pizza today after all. The best part of her job was that Pateena paid her in cash under the counter at the end of every day. She'd have a whole twenty to blow on a Make Me One with Everything pie.

The rest of the afternoon passed without incident, except when Chloe had to hide a pair of faded purple velvet pants she just knew Amy would love. Usually the owner didn't have a problem with employees "saving" items for themselves. Marisol was the coolest boss she'd ever had. She even let Chloe use the shop's machine to hem her own jeans and stuff. But if Lania saw the pants—or liked them herself—she was bound to make trouble. Chloe stashed them under a pile of polyester bowling shirts when she left.

As she approached the restaurant in the damp fog, the windows of Carlucci's glowed like they were lit with gas carriage lanterns, a restaurant out of time. Really, it was just a little Italian pasta place with candles set in old

Chianti bottles like every other little Italian pasta place in the world, but it was hers and Amy's, and it was cozy, and sometimes the insane old owner even remembered them.

When she opened the door, there seemed to be even more candles than usual.

"Happy birthday to you . . . ," Amy sang, wisely giving up after one cracked phrase. Her eager face was lit manically by the glow of seventeen candles around the crust of a Make Me One with Everything pie. "Blow quickly," she added. "Carlucci thinks I'm going to burn the place down."

Chloe laughed with delight, something she couldn't remember doing for days. She took a deep breath.

I wish . . .

I wish . . .

It used to come to her easily: world peace, an end to all of the environmental disasters in the world, the ability to fly, a dog. Wishes seemed to get more complicated as she grew older: for her father to come back. To know who her biological parents were. For a brother or sister. Come to think of it, maybe her recent jonesing was some sort of replacement-male-love sort of thing. *Ewww . . .*

"Chloe?"

She broke out of her reverie.

I wish for a new mountain bike.

No, wait, *world peace.*

She blew, trying not to get spit on their pizza. Chloe saw with amusement that Amy had also pre-ordered the requisite three cans of Nehi grape each.

45

"You're the best, Amy."

"Hey, no problem." They didn't hug; Amy hated things like that. Instead they sat down and began the serious business of shoveling sausage-onion-pepper-tomato-pepperoni-caper-black-olive slices into their mouths as fast as humanly possible. Chloe groaned with pleasure.

"This pizza is the best thing that's happened to me all week. Well, except for last night." She swallowed and looked at Amy, but her friend wasn't biting.

"Yeah? You mean the fall? That *was* some freaky stuff."

"No, afterward. Last night. *After* my mom pulled a major freakage." But Amy really wasn't listening. Chloe sighed, finally giving in to the desperate-to-share, distracted look on her friend's face. "Okay, what's more important than my life on my birthday?"

"Paul and I made out last night!" Amy blurted, suddenly covering her mouth as if she hadn't meant for the words to escape.

Chloe found herself choking. It took half a Nehi to restore normal breathing and swallowing. Of all the things Amy could have said, that was definitely the one she'd least expected. Sure, Amy and Paul had been gazing a bit at each other yesterday—but holy crap, they had all known each other since third grade. It would be like dating a brother. A *really geeky* brother.

"You did *what*?"

"After we took you home, we hung out at his place." Easily pictured: Amy and Paul in his tiny room, surrounded by bookshelves packed with records and his turntable equipment. Lounging on the floor. "I mean, it really freaked us out, you know?" Amy looked her in the eyes. "You really could have died. I mean, the fact that you lived is just— amazing. Like you were given a second chance or something." Chloe silently pleaded that Amy not get into her angel crap; suddenly it was *not* the time. "It sort of, it sounds dumb, a total cliché, but it was just sort of like we realized how death almost touched us. Say things while you can, you know? In case you never get a chance to." She took a deep breath. "So then we were talking about, you know, deep things and life, and uh, then . . . Well, and then . . ."

"You sucked face?"

"Basically, yeah." Was Amy blushing? "But that's not all. I mean, I really care about him, you know? We grew up together, he's like family, so there's like that kind of love, but I never found him sexy before. . . ."

"Oh my God," Chloe said. "Are you telling me you find him sexy *now*? Still? Twenty-four hours later?"

"I don't know. I mean, maybe."

They chewed in silence for a while. Suddenly Chloe's obsession with sexy club guy and flirting with Alyec faded. With Xavier it had been just a kiss, albeit a long and deep one, and if she never saw him again, that was all it would ever be. And Alyec was just a flirt. *This* was serious. This affected the Trio.

If they weren't serious, or if they were and it failed, or if it was just a weirdness from last night and one of

47

them didn't feel as strongly as the other, the once-solid friendship of the three of them was doomed. Chloe didn't relish the thought of being the friend in between after the "divorce." Terribly awkward. Chloe was sure this was going to be a total disaster.

After dinner Amy grabbed for the check when Carlucci left it on the table.

"Will miracles never cease? First I survive the fall and now this . . . ," Chloe said, preemptively ducking. But Amy just frowned a little and walked her home, chattering about Paul the entire time. Only as they neared the Kings' residence did she seem to remember Chloe.

"Was there something you wanted to say before?" she asked.

"Oh, uh, no biggie. I mean, not like *this* biggie." Chloe unlocked the door and pushed it open. "You want to come up? We can—"

There was a crowd of people, well dressed, talking and hanging around the Kings' dining and living room. Hors d'oeuvres were being passed; champagne was being poured into glasses. Paul was there with his parents, and Mr. and Mrs. Scotkin, and other people who were neighbors or familiar faces.

"Oh, crap," her mom said, turning around and seeing her. "Surprise!"

Five

Two glasses of champagne later, Chloe began to enjoy herself. Even though she suspected that the party was some sort of psychological ploy on her mother's behalf to make her daughter feel loved, wanted, and appreciated, she had done an excellent job, and Chloe felt all three. She wondered when her punishment for skipping school and leaving the hospital was going to kick in or if that, too, had been canceled in some sort of amnesty.

Mrs. King could not, however, give up the traditional elements of a birthday party, i.e., an old-fashioned frosted cake and sharing embarrassing photos and pictures of a much younger, and often naked, Chloe.

And of course, a toast.

As soon as her mom began to tap on a glass, Chloe looked around for the quickest way out of being the center of attention. No one was budging; she was trapped.

"As many of you here already know," Mrs. King

began with a sniff, "we aren't exactly sure when Chloe's birthday really is."

Chloe closed her eyes. She was going to do it. She was going to tell the whole story.

The crowd waited expectantly.

"She was born somewhere in the countryside of the old USSR. By the time *we* found her, the only thing the Soviet officials could give us was a document with some scribbles and a sickle-and-star stamp."

Mrs. King pointed to the tattered paper, matted and framed above the dining room table.

"David and I wanted a baby so badly . . . and we were *so* lucky. Chloe was the most beautiful little girl we had ever seen. And she has grown in grace and beauty and intelligence in every way since." Chloe almost groaned aloud. Amy gave her a look, sympathizing with her horror. "And even though we have our little . . . fights, I couldn't be more proud. And if your dad"—*had stuck around*—"were here, he would feel the same way. Chloe, I love you. You're the best thing that has ever happened to me. Happy sixteenth birthday!"

Everyone clinked their glasses and hugged her. Chloe mumbled thanks, just glad that the worst part was over so quickly. As soon as the knot of people around her loosened, she dove for the table of hors d'oeuvres, filled up a plate, and stood in the corner behind a tall plant so she could enjoy the caterer's specialties in peace.

A pair of people walked by, dangerously close. Chloe froze—they didn't seem to have noticed her.

"Remember how badly they were fighting toward the end?" Mrs. Lowe whispered.

"Yes, Anne's toast was so diplomatic," Paul's dad responded. "Considering how he just took off like that."

"Did she ever wind up getting a divorce?"

"No . . . it was like he dropped off the face of the planet. He's never sent a penny for Chloe. Of course," he considered, reflecting, "I don't think Anne or Chloe is suffering."

They were both silent.

"More champagne?" Mrs. Lowe finally suggested.

Chloe chewed contemplatively on a celery stick. Back when her father was still around, when she was young, they also used to celebrate her adoption day, which was just a few weeks later. They hadn't done it since her father left, though.

She left the safety of her plant to try and mingle; the revelers were here for *her*, after all.

"So where's the hired magician?" Paul whispered, approaching her and looking around surreptitiously. "I thought there would be clowns and pony rides and stuff."

"She's not *that* bad," Chloe said, surprising herself with her defense of her mother. It was an amazingly nice little party; one of her mom's friends was playing a cello in the corner, which was kind of weird but lent a sophisticated air to the whole thing. Like they were rich and she was a debutante or something. There was even a little American sturgeon—not endangered, her mother said proudly—caviar. And most importantly, a beautiful white-and-chrome Merida mountain bike with electric pedal assist for the more tiresome hills in San Francisco.

What do you know. I got my wish. She felt a little guilty about the whole world peace thing, though. *Maybe next year.*

Paul was tapping the bottom of his champagne glass nervously.

"Um, Amy told me," Chloe said quietly.

He instantly looked relieved, letting out a deep sigh.

"So you're okay with that?"

"With what?"

"With us . . . having . . . you know . . ."

"Well, no," Chloe said, licking caviar off her fingers. "I mean, seeing as I've had this crush on you since we were nine and—"

"O-*kay*." Paul held up his hand. "That's enough. Message received."

Amy wandered over.

"Hey, guys," she said a little nervously. She and Paul exchanged shy—*shy!*—smiles. Chloe watched their two hands "accidentally" brush each other. Amy smiled, glowing a little. Chloe shuddered a little. *Oh God. Fine. I will be the cool best friend.*

. . .

I will be the cool best friend.

Chloe repeated her little mantra through English the next day as she watched Amy and Paul try very hard not to watch each other. Who cared? Why were they trying to keep it a secret? It wasn't as if anyone in the school actually gave a rat's ass about this particular trio of friends or what went on between them. Mr. Mingrone turned to sketch a giant scarlet *A* on the blackboard. When Amy used the opportunity to toss Paul a note, Chloe put her head down. The plastic desktop reeked of old glue, the sharp tang of pencil lead, and other, less identifiable but equally unpleasant odors, but anything was preferable than watching Paul and Amy.

I will be cool.

Paul was nominally on the school newspaper, which allowed him (and Amy and Chloe) access to the club's better computers and equipment, as well as the old ratty couch and semiprivate room. Almost no one used it until after school, which allowed the three of them to hang there during the day if Paul was around. Chloe decided to use sixth period to catch up on some much-missed sleep.

Chloe knocked tentatively on the ancient, solid-oak door, praying that she wouldn't catch her two best friends making out.

"Come," Paul called, using his Captain Picard voice. Amy was definitely not around.

In fact, when Chloe went in, Paul actually appeared

to be working on the paper, sitting on the edge of his desk and looking over an article.

"Crunchy cheese-baked scrod every Wednesday for the next *month*." He sighed, throwing down the lunch schedule. It was Paul, Amy, and Chloe's private opinion that the only reason anyone read *The Lantern* was for the cafeteria menu and Sabrina Anne's often-banned column.

"Why don't you get your mom to pack a lunch? PB and kimchi. Breakfast of champions." Chloe threw her book bag, and then herself, onto the couch.

"Yeah, right." Paul kicked his legs under the desk.

It was strange having him look down on her like that. Or maybe it was just an overall change in his demeanor since the whole hooking-up-with-Amy thing. He seemed calm and confident, like he was relaxing on a throne instead of perched on a desk. Actually, he looked pretty good today. He was wearing a simple black T-shirt and baggy jeans that complemented his square, compact body better than any of the bowling shirts or DJ wear he often sported.

Uh, what? Chloe suddenly realized she was *admiring* Paul's looks. Good ol' Paul, with the harelip scar that tugged his mouth when he smiled. *Kind of endearing, really . . .*

Chloe shook herself.

"So what's been going on?" she asked quickly.

"Between you almost dying and Amy? Not a whole lot." He looked at her with faint amusement in his dark brown eyes. Chloe felt her palms sweat. It was a small room, secluded from the rest of the high school; their aloneness was a very palpable third presence in the room with them.

It's just because Amy likes him, she told herself. *A competition thing.* In the still air of the room she could just smell the deodorant and soap he used and underneath, a saltiness that she realized was probably his skin. The way he was sitting there, it would be so easy just to walk over and push herself against him; they would be the same height. She could wrap her arms around his neck like she had with Xavier and pull him in—

"Robble robble, blah blah blah—hey, King, you listening?"

"Yes!" She leapt up, trying to shake off the desire. "No. I mean, I gotta go. I, uh, forgot to hand in my essay to Mingrone—shit, I hope he hasn't left yet."

She grabbed her bag and made for the door.

"I think he said we have until tomorrow," Paul called after her. The door slammed between them.

I will be cool.

Yeah, right.

At work Chloe forced herself to seriously look over every guy who came in. Including a few who were gay. Things were very bad indeed when she found herself almost kissing her best friend. Who seemed to be her other best friend's boyfriend.

Marisol didn't help anything by putting the Eurythmics'

55

"I Need a Man" on the shop speakers. Chloe jumped guiltily when she heard the chorus.

"Is it that obvious?"

"Honey, you're *dripping* hormones all over my nice clean floor." The older woman smiled at her. Chloe wished her mom was more like her manager. She always seemed to understand Chloe's moods immediately and unless there was a sale coming up, was often ready to talk and listen.

"Who put on this old shit?" Lania screamed from the shoe section, hands over her ears in horror.

Chloe and Marisol exchanged "what can you do" looks. "Go get yourself a boy, girl. You're not concentrating; it's obvious your attention is elsewhere," Marisol said in a lighthearted voice.

As Chloe patiently ripped through the hem seams of more jeans, she reflected on what her boss had said. Maybe she *could* get it "out of her system." Maybe she was due for a nice boyfriend.

Or a visit to Xavier.

Once Chloe had found the right street, she pulled the crumpled card out of her back pocket. *I'm going to have to get better at this.* She imagined herself in a business suit, somewhere in a steel-and-glass future, shaking someone's hand and pulling out her own card, all rumpled and greasy. She checked the address against the building. Xavier must have had a little money or have been crashing with a friend who did: it was a *nice* old house, three floors, dark wood and bay windows on a street with soft green trees and no traffic. Of course, both sides of the street were stuffed with parked cars—rich neighborhood or not, this was still San Francisco.

The front door was propped open and there was a hand-scrawled note to FedEx posted over the buzzer. The lobby smelled of lemon wood cleaner. There was only one apartment per floor; Xavier had the attic. With gables. Chloe had always dreamed of living in a real old house like this instead of her bug-ugly vinyl-sided ranch. She climbed the stairs, letting her hand trail along the smoothly polished rail.

But in the half-light of the stairwell Chloe began to question what she was doing: going to some foreign older guy's apartment by herself at twilight without anyone knowing where she was. He could turn out to be anything: a rapist or murderer. A vampire, even.

She paused briefly, but an image of herself kissing Paul pushed her forward. *I won't go in. I'll stand in the hallway and ask him if he wants to go out. Maybe grab a coffee.*

His door was dark wood with molding and a little brass-and-glass peephole at eye height. She raised her hand to knock . . .

And realized the door was pushed open just the slightest bit.

"Uh, hello?" she called out, stepping back.

"*Help . . . ,*" a choked, wheezy voice called from inside. "*Help me!*"

Chloe hesitated on the doorstep. It could be a trap. He could kidnap girls and rape them and sell them into slavery and . . .

"*Please . . . someone . . .*"

Chloe pushed open the door and stepped inside.

The apartment smelled of sickness and decay, which was strange against the clean, antique furniture and expensive, modern lighting. In each gable was a carefully designed nook for reading and sitting—*just like I would have done.* Chloe made herself follow the sound of wheezing.

Lying under the lintel to the bathroom was a very different Xavier.

He was wearing the same clothes from the club two nights ago, but they were torn and pulled like he had tried to rip them off his body. His face had bubbled up like the rind of a diseased grapefruit. His cheeks and forehead were swollen and red, with white liquid, lymph or pus, oozing out of giant sores.

"*Help—*" He was trying to scream, but his throat was swollen so badly, he could barely breathe. He groaned and twisted, trying to crawl out of his skin. He flopped onto his stomach and Chloe got a look at his back. Long, oozing cankers and welts, like claw marks. Exactly where she had scratched and kneaded him outside the club.

Chloe backed up slowly.

Must call.

Without thought, like she was walking through syrup, Chloe found the handset of a cordless phone in the living room, resting on top of one of those expensive giant HEPA filters from Sharper Image, like the one her mom had. She dialed 911.

She recited the address when a brusque, disinterested voice came on. "There's someone here. Covered in sores. Can barely breathe. It looks like he's dying."

It looks like he's dying.

"We'll be right there, ma'am. What's your telephone number?"

"I don't—" She looked at the card and gave them his cell. After hanging up she went back to Xavier. He was hissing and coughing and his eyes were crusty and half shut. She wondered if he could see her, if he would recognize her.

Exactly where she had scratched him.

Chloe waited until she heard sirens approaching, and then she ran.

Six

Friday passed normally, and Xavier wasn't mentioned in any obits or police beats, so Chloe was determined to have a normal weekend, too. Hormone free. Guy free. Falls-from-towers and formerly-hot-now-sick-strangers free.

She got up on Saturday, poured herself a big box of Lucky Charms, and watched new (really crappy) cartoons for a couple of hours. It was sunny out, so she drew the shades, just like she used to when she was young so she wouldn't be tempted to leave the glowing light of the television for the great outdoors.

At two she met Amy at Relax Now. Chloe had casually suggested to Amy the night before that they treat themselves to manicures with some of her birthday money. Amy objected at first, calling it a middle-class, bourgeois ritual of the Burberry-knockoff set. Chloe told her to cut the crap and enjoy it; they had never done it before and might never do it again. Besides, she was paying.

And Amy actually seemed pretty cheerful, looking over her nails as they dried. She had talked the most artistic seeming of the women there into painting the lower half of all her nails black, then putting a single clawlike black stripe in the middle of each one. She flexed and re-flexed her fingers under the little lamps.

"Grrr," she said.

Chloe was still having hers worked on. She'd opted for the hot paraffin, vitamin-wrap, extra-super-cleany options and was drilling the woman doing it with a battery of questions: Could fingernails be dirty even if they didn't look it? Could you carry diseases under your nails? What about toxic fungi?

"Yes, yes, and yes," the woman replied, zealously buffing. "I knew a girl once, she went to a place—not here, a *dirty* place—she got a pedicure and had to have her whole toe removed afterward. Nasty infection. Anyway, this will take care of all that. You could eat with them now."

Chloe felt relieved. And guilty. She hoped Xavier was okay. She had to somehow check on him later.

It *was* kind of funny, though, that she'd managed to spread something diseaselike to her partner before she'd ever even had sex. Funny in a loose sense of the word, of course.

"This is *perfect*," Amy said, admiring her nails. "We're going to the Temple of Arts tonight—this will freak the shit out of all the vampire role players there."

"Cool. I haven't been there in so long." Chloe didn't have anything planned for that evening, except for cooking with her mother (mother-daughter time), something she was anxious to get out of. And it would be an excellent way to get over whatever weird rush she'd felt with Paul earlier that week. The three of them just hanging out would be a good thing. "I promised Mom I'd help her with some weird and complicated recipe tonight, but I should be done by nine or ten."

"Oh." Amy stared more intently at her nails, blushing. "I meant, like, just me and Paul. Like a date."

"Like a *date*?" It had been just a casual, high-tension kissing session before. . . . When had their status changed? "Oh." Chloe fidgeted, prompting a smack from the woman working on her. "Oh. That's cool. No problem."

I will be the cool friend.

"How about tomorrow? We could totally get together tomorrow," Amy suggested eagerly.

"Nah. I'm taking my new bike for a ride." Disappointment and embarrassment and anger raged through her brain, making it difficult to sound casual.

"All day?"

"Yeah," Chloe said firmly, staring at her nails. *"All day."*

At home Chloe began to feel bad about breaking her "I will be cool" mantra when Amy obviously was already embarrassed by the whole discussion. And she had kind of acted like a baby. Of course she and Paul wanted

63

to spend time together. They were *dating*, dummy.

Chloe finally e-mailed:

You wanna hang Sunday night? Rent a movie or something . . . xo, C.

That didn't stop her from being grumpy about it, though. Chloe drowsed on her bed, visions of Xavier, Alyec, and—yuck—Paul spinning around in her head before her mom finally demanded her help with dinner. She was silent in the kitchen.

"Is something wrong, Chloe?" Her mother was in a rare, selfless good mood.

"No." She smashed a clove of garlic with the side of her knife for emphasis.

Her mom looked at her sideways but didn't say anything.

Dinner was fabulous if weird, as all of her mom's Saturday night attempts tended to be. While Mrs. King napped on the couch in the living room afterward, Chloe channel flipped, pausing at some sort of nighttime soap she never would have normally given a second thought to, but a handsome couple was making out on the beach at night. Chloe watched them wistfully, imagining sand under her own head and lips against hers.

"How was your bike ride, Chlo?" Amy asked in line for lunch on Monday.

"It was great." It really had been. And if she hadn't been so preoccupied with how pissed she was at Paul

64

and Amy and how she really wanted her own boyfriend, it would have been perfect. She had never noticed how many goddamn happy couples there were all across San Francisco before. Making out in public. Everywhere.

She felt in her pocket for a quarter that wasn't there and tried to find something interesting in what the lunch hag was doing. "You never replied to my e-mail."

"Sorry about that," Amy continued bravely. "My phone ran out of juice. I didn't get the message until this morning."

"No problem." Chloe realized she couldn't watch the pot of reddish glop—"chili"—being stirred around by the woman with the mustache. The beans looked suspiciously like cockroaches. She turned her head, but there was nothing else to look at in the small line but Amy.

"You—you want to hang after school today?" Amy got her like a deer in headlights. Her big eyes were trembling: *I'm really sorry,* they said. "I suck, I know."

Chloe resisted.

"Please? I'll make it up to you. You and me and Paul, we'll go watch the sea lions, like we used to. I'll buy you an ice cream. *Please?*"

Chloe couldn't help smiling. This was Amy, after all. "Oh, all right. But I want two flavors, swirled."

"You're on!" Amy agreed, grinning.

Whap—their moment of reconciliation was interrupted by a pile of red mush hitting Chloe's tray with a sickening, definitely unfoodlike sound.

"Next!" the lunch lady screamed.

As she and Amy left the lunch line, they ran smack into Alyec.

"King!" he said, smiling. "When are we going to hang out?"

Chloe watched his curvy, exotic lips. Smiling at *her.*

"This afternoon? My friends and I are going to go down to the pier and watch the sea lions. Want to come?" Amy looked askance at her, surprised.

It was the lamest, lamest thing she could have ever imagined saying to Alyec. But when the words came out of her mouth, they were confident, and she looked him in the eye.

Alyec raised his eyebrows; it really did sound corny. "Sea lions, eh? Well, why not? It's free."

"It's a date," Chloe said casually as she headed off to a table. Amy trailed, her mouth hanging open.

Paul and Amy were trying to behave, Chloe could see that.

Amy was sitting on his lap in the glowy late-afternoon sunshine, contented smiles on her and Paul's faces. There was no actual making out going on. *So why do I feel like vomiting?*

"Arp!" a sea lion barked.

She licked her cone, using her tongue to carefully pick up the chocolate with an equal amount of vanilla.

The bay was dark blue and the bridge an ancient,

rusty red. Little islands in the distance faded in and out of view as strings of perfect sailboats floated in front of them. The crowds of tourists weren't even that bad.

It was almost perfect. Almost. Alyec wasn't here.

And why should he be? Why should anything I want ever work out? Come on, this was *Alyec*—as Paul said, "He is steely-eyed, chisel-faced young Russian." Why would he show up for a lame ass double date with three of the out crowd?

"Hey, look at that one!" Paul wasn't pointing at a sea lion; he was pointing at one of the few tourists. But this one was a beaut: he wore a hat that said Frisco on it and a T-shirt that said Alcatraz and was trying to take a picture of the pier with a tiny, bright yellow disposable camera.

It was the most exciting thing that had happened since they came.

And now the sun was beginning to set. The night ocean breezes picked up, brushing a strand of dark hair into Chloe's face. She brushed it out of the way impatiently.

"You wanna go somewhere, get coffee?" Paul asked eventually.

Chloe sighed. *Ah, I am now officially a third wheel.*

"Where are the sea lions? Or are you talking about the fat tourists?"

Chloe spun around. Alyec was walking up the pier,

hands in his pockets, frowning as he tried to make out the animals in the dimming light.

"Over there." She pointed casually at the water. It took every ounce of her will not to jump up and shout his name joyfully. *I am cool,* she repeated, finally for a different reason. He was drop-dead-gorgeous casual tonight, button-down open over a T-shirt, no socks. The approaching dusk made his blond hair look like it was streaked with honey and brown.

"Oh! I see them now!" He actually looked interested; his face lit up. "Very cool. We didn't have any of those in St. Petersburg. Or maybe once we did, but they were all eaten."

Chloe introduced Amy and Paul. Alyec shook their hands formally. "Amy—I think I saw you at that café with the chicken. You were reading some of your poetry?"

Paul looked a little annoyed. Amy blushed. "I do some readings now and then."

There was a long, awkward pause. A single sea lion noiselessly slipped into the water. Others soon began to follow.

"Well, this was fun," Alyec said, looking around. "But maybe we should do something else now? It's getting too dark to see the lions."

Chloe tried not to giggle. It sounded so cute coming out that way.

"We were going to get coffee," Paul said.

"Okay. Then what?"

"A club?" Amy suggested.

"Excellent!" Alyec pointed at her like she had just picked the correct amount for a washer on *The Price Is Right*. Then he looked serious. "The one thing I really miss about my old town is the dancing. Every night, if you wanted. No cover, either."

"I don't know about going dancing tonight—" Whatever Paul's reasons were, they were cut off by a sharp jab in the side from Amy's elbow.

"Sounds great," she said. "Chloe?"

"Absolutely." She imagined dancing with Alyec like she had with Xavier. Then she thought of Xavier in the parking lot and Xavier on the floor of his apartment, covered in sores. She beat the guilt down as fast as she could. "Um . . . anywhere but the Bank!"

Alyec, Paul, and Amy all looked at her.

"It sucks on a Monday night," Chloe continued lamely. *And Tuesday and Wednesday and Thursday and Friday*. In fact, she would be happy if she never went back there again.

To Chloe's relief they settled on the Raven, a place that played a lot of good dance music but didn't have a dance floor. What they *did* have was a lot of comfy old couches and a tendency to serve to those who were underage. Also a dartboard, which Alyec and Paul instantly commandeered.

"Look at them," Amy said, giggling. Paul was closing one eye and aiming. Alyec had his arms crossed and a serious expression on his brow. "They're like cavemen."

"I don't think Cro-Magnon men used darts to bring down woolly mammoths." Chloe sipped delicately from her Hoegaarden. Alyec was impressed by her choice but hadn't offered to buy it for her. Which was a shame, since it was five bucks.

"I think he fits in well," Amy said, meaning Alyec and the trio of friends.

"I don't want him to fit in well," Chloe said with a little more passion than she meant. "I want him to come over here, drag me outside, and kiss me like he really means it." She took a couple of big gulps.

"Oh my God, Chloe gets shallow. You really *do* want a handsome caveman."

"I like talking," Chloe protested. "Talking is good. Later. *After* the making out."

"Well." Alyec sat down next to her, coming over the back of the couch. "I have taught your friend a little lesson in the finer points of losing."

Paul just growled and sat next to Amy, who turned so she could lean on his lap. Alyec put his arm behind Chloe on the back of the couch, touching her occasionally to emphasize points. She wondered if he realized that he was driving her crazy. *Probably. That's how he wound up with a crowd of worshipers in the first place, isn't it?* Chloe made a mental note that no matter what

70

happened, she would not end up in that category. Chloe was different from them, the Keiras and the Halley Dietrichs of the world.

Paul challenged Alyec to darts twice more, never winning. Amy panhandled for jukebox quarters. Chloe watched Alyec, sipped her beer, and occasionally moderated Amy's music decisions. At ten Amy's mom called and insisted she come home from whatever scandalous thing she was doing. All four parted ways at the street corner outside, but Alyec didn't offer to see Chloe home.

"See you in Am civ tomorrow," Alyec said. "Thanks for inviting me out today." He kissed her lightly on the cheek, then turned and disappeared into the night.

It was nice. A *nice* kiss. Very *nice*. Too *nice*.

Chloe felt like screaming.

"You could just wear a T-shirt that says I'm Easy," Amy suggested.

In the end, Chloe was glad to walk home by herself. The air was dry and a little chill, just the way fall weather should be. Quick little winds pushed leaves around and around on the pavement, making dry scratchy noises. Clouds skittered across the moon. *Very Halloweeny.* For the first time in days her thoughts drifted away from Xavier, her fall, and even Alyec: she wondered what Amy would do for a costume this year. They were always spectacular, complicated, and often puns: last year she'd been a Big Mac Daddy, with a red wig, clown shoes, and gold chains. Paul had worn jeans and a jean jacket with a pin of a DNA helix that said Selfish Gene. Chloe had just worn a vintage evening gown and a half mask, one that Amy had helped her take apart and put on a stick so she would look like a Venetian attending a ball.

"Hey—*smile*, sister!"

Chloe broke out of her reverie to see one of San Francisco's many friendly street people approaching her. He was tall and probably in his twenties, with blond hair in stupid white-man dreads. His clothes were grubby. Chloe forced a smile at him and kept walking.

"Hey, sister, can you spare a dollar or two?" He ran alongside her and put out his hand. "I really need a beer." He flashed a toothy grin at her. His honesty was refreshing—and amusing—but Chloe suddenly realized there was no one else on the street with them, and all of the shops were closed for the night.

Her Spidey sense, as Paul would have called it, tingled. She picked up the pace.

"Sorry," she said.

"Come *on*." He grabbed at her hand. "You gotta have a dollar or two. Everyone does."

Chloe pulled her hand away. "I'm sorry, I don't."

"I'll bet you do." He grabbed her harder and spun her around.

"Let go of me!" She yelled it, looking him right in the eye, just like they had taught her in the self-defense class she and her mom had taken. He put his other hand over her mouth. It stank of old body, dog, and pee.

"Come on, don't be like that. We can have a little fun." He leered at her.

Suddenly she was *angry*, all fear gone. Rage burned in her: who did he think he was? What gave him the right to do this to *her*—to anyone?

Chloe bit down on his hand, catching a thick piece of palm meat. She ground her teeth down and pulled back her head, ripping something loose.

"Holy *shit*—mother*fucker*!" He pulled that hand away, stared at it dumbly, thick ropes of blood gushing out of it. Then he whacked her in the face.

It hurt *bad*. Chloe didn't care. She spun around. Using his hand to balance herself, Chloe leapt up and kicked him on the chest.

Which was odd, because she didn't know a single martial art, and she'd actually been aiming for his crotch.

He stumbled backward, winded.

Chloe waited.

"You little—" He dove at her.

She leapt easily out of the way and grabbed his hair as he passed. She yanked back hard on it so he lost balance, then spun and kicked him in the side as he fell. She channeled all her rage at the world, at her friends, at Alyec, at her dad who'd left her, at her bad chemistry grade into that kick. There was a very satisfying sound of ribs breaking. He rolled onto his stomach and she kicked him on his other side.

"Fucking—bitch—," he wheezed. "I'll kill you—"

Chloe backhanded him on the side of the head. He went out immediately. Blood trickled out of his ear and down his jaw.

She stood there, panting. *What now? Call 911 anonymously for the second time in a week?*

Nah. He didn't deserve it. She turned and started walking home.

The night was the same as it was when she began her walk: beautiful, cold, and quiet. Chloe whistled a little tune, still full of adrenaline, realizing something strange.

She had enjoyed *every second* of the fight.

Seven

Her mother didn't come home until late that night, after she was home and asleep, so Chloe was spared the almost inevitable confrontation about the bruises and scrapes on her cheeks. She slept dreamlessly until her alarm rang and managed to hide her face from her mom until she got out of the house.

"What the hell happened to *you*?" It was blunt, but at least Amy didn't start off with any is-your-mom-hitting-you bullshit. She was smoking a clove cigarette this morning, trying to look cool by casually dropping it and stepping on it as they approached the school.

"I walked into a door. *Again*," Chloe answered tragically.

Amy hit her.

"I was attacked by a bum last night, walking home." She wasn't sure if it was a good idea to tell the truth, but after not bothering to mention her night at the club *or* Xavier, Chloe was beginning to feel uncomfortable with the number of omissions and half lies she was telling her friend.

"Oh my God. Are you *okay*? Wait, what am I saying. This is the Chloe King who survived a fall from Coit Tower." Amy raised one eyebrow and shook her head.

"I beat the living shit out of him," Chloe couldn't help bragging.

"Yeah? Which episode of *Buffy* was that? Or more importantly, what was he on?"

"Hey! I attribute it to my awesome strength, lightning-fast reflexes, and that self-defense course I aced."

"Uh-huh," Amy said, nodding and pretending to agree. "So. What was he on?"

Why didn't Ame believe her? Was it so unbelievable that she'd managed to defend herself successfully from an attacker? Chloe thought back on the fight. The man had been large, six-foot two or so, but skinny. He had obviously been living on the streets for a while. She tried to play the scene through Amy's eyes. It seemed believable, almost like a scenario from the self-defense class—up until, with no training, she's done that high kick onto his chest. And instead of running away, she had finished the fight.

Chloe sighed. "Probably smack or something."

The predictable appearance of crunchy cheese-baked scrod on Wednesday was a surprisingly reassuring thing. Though it made Chloe want to retch, lunch seemed to indicate that everything was normal. Sure, Amy and

Paul tended to disappear from the scene every available moment—Chloe was convinced that someday one of the face-sucking couples she passed in the hall before class would turn out to be them. She'd taken to walking between classes faster, head down.

Amy *did* manage to find five minutes on the walk between school and work on Wednesday to talk, bringing a latte for her friend, the first of many what Chloe called "gilfts": guilt gifts. They chatted about this and that, but it was always the same problem.

Chloe wanted to *talk* about things—like the fall. Like her fight with the bum. Like Xavier, for Christ's sake. But she and Amy had been so apart recently that it took a few minutes of rapid reacquainting before Chloe felt comfortable enough to *really* talk, and by then one of them—usually Amy—always had to leave.

At Pateena's, Marisol had turned on the old black-and-white television—one of four throughout the store that played trippy visuals to trance on the speakers. Some dumb sitcom was playing while she set up the tapes. Chloe absently watched it while taking her break, scanning the obituaries again, looking for Xavier. The TV show was something about a normal guy and his hippie wife and the comic mayhem that ensued as a result of their differences.

Chloe suddenly envisioned a different version of her mother: a slightly ditzier, San Francisco hippie version who dragged her daughter to horrible things like drumming circles and Goddess nights. Maybe she owned a bookstore. She would be kooky but easy to talk to and would have relevant things to say about boys when Chloe opened up to her over a mug of homemade chai. Nothing negative. Nothing like "don't date them," for instance.

From what little she remembered and had been told, her dad was more that type of person. A modern do-gooder, a legal defense aide who worked with immigrants by day and took his wife to benefits and galas for nonprofits by night. Chloe tried to picture him at Carlucci's with her, the gray and hazy areas of his face pieced in with old scrapbook photos. He would tell her that boys were terrible things and that he should know, because he had been one. He would blush but try to remain supportive when she talked about Xavier. He would be interested that Alyec was Russian. He should be, considering it had been *his* idea to adopt the orphan of an ex-Soviet state. Right now Chloe felt like she had *no one* to talk to.

"Hey."

A pair of black knit kitty cat ears appeared above the rack where she was working. The guy wearing them stood on his toes and waved at her.

"Hey," she said, smiling.

"I think I'm going to buy a whole *suit* this time," he said. "Or maybe just a jacket," he added.

"Lania is our queer-eye-for-every-person girl. She

can help you pick out something professional *and* stellar if you don't mind the constant bitching."

"Oh." In the flash of sunlight his eyes were almost green and very deep, like an expensive glass paperweight.

Chloe desperately tried to think of some way of continuing the conversation.

"Hey, um, I think I want the pattern for your hat after all," she said. "My friend Amy knits, and she owes me a birthday present."

"Oh! Absolutely!" He gave up his tippy-toe routine, seeming to suddenly realize he could simply walk around the rack. He wore a dark green shirt with jeans and black square-tipped European-looking shoes. Very much the clove cigarette type: dark and mysterious. His shoulders were larger than they had seemed the other day, and he held a copy of James Joyce's *Ulysses* under his arm. "I'll bring it by."

"Sure, that would be great."

There was a silence between them for a moment.

"Or," he added, "I could take you out for a coffee after work sometime and give it to you."

Chloe smiled. "*That* would be great."

"How 'bout tomorrow?"

"Absolutely!"

"I'm Brian, uh, by the way."

"I'm Chloe. Pleased to meet you." She made a serious look and held out her hand. He shook it.

"Chloe—like 'Daphnis and Chloe,' the Greek myth?"

"One and the same," Chloe said, surprised he knew of it.

"You know," he said, glancing at the newspaper section she held, "not everyone who dies winds up in the obituaries."

"What? Oh." She blushed, thinking furiously. "I—I guess I'm just morbid. I, uh, like to see how old people are when they die and stuff."

"Try the crossword instead," he suggested, smiling. "It looks impressive and high-falutin' when you do it with a pen."

Chloe grinned. "Maybe I'll just do that."

She stayed late to help Marisol lock up, checking her watch nervously. Now that the new season of television had once again begun, Wednesdays were *Smallville* and takeout night, her mother's attempt to connect to her daughter via cable's younger generation. One of her more successful attempts, actually, since Chloe loved dumplings and Michael Rosenbaum. Plus since the unexpected birthday party she and her mom seemed to be getting along better, something Chloe didn't want to screw up.

By the time she helped Marisol pull the chain gate down, it was seven forty-five. There was *no way* the bus was going to get her home in time. Three miles on the bus took forever.

"Here." Marisol handed her a ten-dollar bill.

"I only stayed an extra hour," Chloe protested.

"Shush!" The older woman pushed it into her hand and closed her fist around it. "Take a cab home. I got a ten-year-old, and someday she's going to be your age. It freaks me out watching you and Lania. Be safe."

"You have a daughter?" Chloe felt twice as embarrassed taking the money now, having just found out about an important part of her boss's life that she knew nothing of before.

"Yeah. She's at her dad's this week. Lazy son of a bitch loves his little girl, at least. See you tomorrow." Marisol tossed her long brown-black hair over her shoulder like a younger woman, like a girl, like someone who didn't have a ten-year-old and an ex-husband and a business. When she crossed the street, she kind of bounced.

Chloe looked at the ten in her hand and thought about the differences between her mom and her boss, and the little ten-year-old she hadn't known about until today, who split her life between her parents. Like Paul now. Chloe didn't even have that option.

She looked around: the streets were devoid of regular cars, let alone cabs. The faintest curl of cold air hit her nose, sharp and electric. When it faded, Chloe noticed the city-made warmth, the biological smell of trees and dirt and humans, men and women running about and excited, glad the workday was over.

Chloe began to trot, methodically jogging like she

did in gym to do as little work as possible and not get noticed. Her breasts bounced uncomfortably in her not-designed-for-jogging bra.

Then, without thinking, she opened up her stride and *ran*.

She ran like her body had been waiting its whole life to actually run, as if she had been held in check up until this moment. She didn't even have to think about the movement of her arms or the placement of her feet and legs the way Mr. Parmalee was always shouting. She ran with wide steps, eating up the vanilla slabs of concrete below with hungry feet. And when her steps weren't wide enough—she leapt.

Houses passed in a blur, parked cars looked like they were moving. She jumped over fire hydrants and small bushes, not like a normal long or high jumper, but springing with her arms held curled at her sides to break her fall if she mislanded.

She never did.

When she crossed the street, she did it in the middle of the block and leapt onto the hood of a car that blocked the pedestrian walkway. She was gratified to hear the alarm go off in whoops. From there she found herself using a *parking meter* as a step closer down to the sidewalk, her left foot delicately resting on it for a moment while her right foot reached for the ground.

The energy, strength, and speed she felt were just like in the fight with the homeless guy—but they lasted longer. Not just an adrenaline burst. And there was no rage, no flight or fight—just the pure joy of movement, of almost flying through the deserted night.

She cut through an empty lot, pretty sure it was a faster route home. Even though there was no moon that night and no streetlights in the area, she managed to leap over dead tires, puddles of broken glass, and unpleasant-looking plants without nicking herself on a single obstacle.

When she finally leapt up the steps to her house and let herself in, she wasn't even winded.

"Just in time," her mother said, smiling. She was laying out cartons of Chinese.

The clock on the TV said 7:57.

Eight

"Hey, Alyec," Chloe called, waving to him across the hallway the next morning.

"Hey, King." He waved back, but he turned around to continue his conversation with Keira. Chloe could almost *feel* Keira's smugness as he dismissed her. It was infuriating. Chloe slunk away as if she had never stopped. Yeah, she should probably be happy about Brian. But Alyec was *hot*. Sexy. Drop-dead gorgeous. Covetousness inspiring. She snuck one look back to watch his wheat blond hair (or was it rye? What did they grow in Russia?) fall over his brow in waves like the fringe on an expensive pillow. *Maybe I should tell him that I'm a Ruskie, too.*

Or maybe, she thought, maybe she should choose one guy and stick with him. Either pursue Alyec or continue with Brian.

Nah . . . this is way more fun.

"Hey." Paul waved at her from the river of teenage

traffic that was going the opposite way, down the left side of the hall. He jumped into a free space next to her. "Take any long falls from tall buildings lately?"

"I base-dived the Transamerica—does that count?"

"We were thinking about going to the arcade at Sony later," he continued. *And since when did he and Amy become a "we"? Amy and she were a "we." Amy, Paul, and she were a "we."* Should she just assume from now on that whenever either one of her best friends used that pronoun, they were only referring to themselves? "Wanna come?"

Oh, now I'm being invited *places by them. Pity the third wheel.*

"No thanks, I've got plans." She didn't know if hazel eyes could look cold, but she tried her best, making her face go flat with lack of emotion. She had practiced it in front of a mirror. The expression looked good with her high cheekbones.

"Plans?" Paul asked. His eyebrows raised almost to his spiked bangs.

"Yeah, *plans*. Maybe another time."

And she walked away.

Of course, she knew it wouldn't drop like that; she was *hoping* it wouldn't. It came during math in the form of a single-character text message on her phone from Amy: *?*

She responded: *thanks 4 the invite, tho.*

Amy: *whats ur prob biyatch? @ least come to my reading fri 7 @ b. rooster Puhlleeeeeeeezzze :) ! ucan bring alyec.*

86

Yeah, right, if she wanted to make sure that Alyec never wanted to hang out with her or her friends again. Amy's poetry could have that effect on people.

Chloe put away her phone, not wanting to deal.

Brian showed up at Pateena's precisely at six.

Chloe was leaning in the doorway, carefully searching through the obituaries. No mention of Xavier. "Where to?" Chloe asked, shoving the paper into her bag.

He seemed to have dressed up a little. His pants were something soft, black, and matte that almost looked like velvet. Wool? Velour? Chloe found herself resisting the urge to reach out and feel it. *I wonder if he likes dancing. . . .*

"I was thinking . . . the zoo." He looked at her expectantly, his brown eyes wide.

"The *zoo*?" Mugs of coffee and an intimate dinner melted away. "Isn't it closed?"

"Nope. Not until eight. And I'm a member, so we get in free."

The zoo . . . Come to think of it, she hadn't been there in years, even though it was reasonably close by. And no one had ever offered to take her there before.

"All right, but you're buying me a souvenir drink cup."

"Hey, *you're* the one with a job."

"*You're* the one who asked me out."

"Touché," he admitted. He was so easy to talk to! This was, like, their third conversation and they were

87

already bantering like old friends. "Okay, one souvenir drink cup for you. But if you felt like the evening went well, I wouldn't object to you purchasing a stuffed monkey for *me*."

Chloe grinned. "It's a deal."

There were no crowds outside the zoo gates, only families leaving, and all Brian had to do was wave his card at the guard and point to Chloe and they waltzed in. So much better than the heat, lines, and crowds she remembered from experiences there as a kid. It was also kind of cool going there at dusk: the overhanging trees gathered shadows under them, making the place seem more wild.

"Are you in college?" she finally asked casually, looking at a map. He didn't look *that* much older than her. . . .

"Not yet. I'm taking a couple of years off."

"So, what did you need that suit for?"

"Twenty questions!" he said, laughing. "I'm looking to major in zoology. Hence, uh, the zoo. But that's kind of a difficult program for an undergrad degree, and competition is fierce. I wasn't exactly a . . . *scholar* in high school, so I thought I would get some experience by working at a zoo or animal rescue league or something like that. I'm in the interviewing process right now. You'd be surprised how many people want crappy, low-paying jobs that involve shoveling a lot of animal—well, *crap*."

Chloe smiled. "Sounds cool to me . . . I've never had

88

a pet more interesting than a goldfish or a beta. My mom's allergic."

"I have four cats," he said smugly, watching her envy. "Tabitha, Sebastian, Sabrina, and Agatha."

"Four?"

"Oh, that's nothing. When I was little, we had . . ." But his brow furrowed, and he looked away distractedly.

"When you were little . . . ?" Chloe prompted him.

"We had a lot. Of pets," he finished lamely. "Lots of cats. Rare breeds, too, like Cornish rex and Maine coon."

They wandered the paths randomly. Chloe *loved* seeing the zoo like this, for free, with no pressure to see all of the top animals, to see every square inch before it was time to go. They could pause as long as they wanted to watch a pair of simple mallard ducks that wandered into the aviary and skip the exhibits they didn't care about without feeling guilty.

But Brian was much quieter than before, except when he was pointing out interesting factoids and habits of the various animals they saw. He chewed the inside of his lip when he thought she wasn't looking, as if trying to decide whether or not to say more.

"So you had lots of pets when you were young?" Chloe prompted when they stopped to get her a diet Coke in a plastic monkey-shaped cup. He ordered one of those cappuccinos from a machine, something Chloe wouldn't have done if she were *starving*.

"Yeah, uh . . ." Brian's face fell, completely losing the animation it had when he was talking about the meerkats and the cassowaries. "My mom's dead," he finally said. "And my dad and me—we don't really get along. He's got this apartment he keeps here in the city—where I live, for now—but he does a lot of work out of his other house in Sausalito. We don't talk much."

He shook his head. "But that's *way* too much information for a first date. You probably just want to make sure I'm not some kind of freak."

Chloe laughed. "I have a secret mouse," she volunteered, lightening the mood.

"What?"

"A secret mouse. His name is Mus-mus. From the Latin name for mouse, you know? *Mus musculus.* My mom doesn't know I keep him in a drawer of my bureau."

"You keep a *mouse*? In your *bureau*?"

"Yeah," she said a little defensively. "Mom wouldn't let me otherwise."

"That's so . . . cute." He looked at her in wonder, as if that was the most charming thing anyone had ever said. They wandered out of the concession area, Chloe sucking noisily on the straw that impaled the monkey's head. A sign pointed to penguins, otters, and lions.

"Hey . . . ," Chloe said, remembering bits of the dream she'd had after she fell off the tower. "Let's go see the lions. I . . . dreamt about some recently. . . ."

"Yeah?"

"Yeah." She looked down as they walked, trying to match her stride to his, but Brian's legs were much longer. "My dad's gone, too," she said. "And my mom's kind of a bitch."

"*Every*one's mom is a bitch when you're sixteen." He laughed. "I just would have liked to have known mine."

"How did you know I was sixteen?" Chloe asked, suddenly suspicious.

"I didn't." He shrugged. "It was more of a general comment. Not you in particular, but when 'you're' sixteen, meaning everyone."

He took the tiniest sip from his cappuccino but still managed to get a foamy mustache.

"The day after I turned sixteen, I almost punched my dad out," Brian continued. He straightened up and looked her in the eye, daring her to disbelieve him.

"That would be *so* much more effective if you didn't have milk all over your lip," she said, laughing. She reached over with a napkin and carefully wiped it off, trying not to drag it across his mouth too hard. She was doubly glad she had a manicure: it made the gesture twice as sexy. Denim dust under the nails would *not* have been attractive.

He blushed, and his hand went through his hair, dislodging a lock that made a Superman-style curl in the middle of his forehead. *With glasses and a dye job, he'd make a very passable Clark Kent.*

He's so . . . cute*!* Chloe thought again, and it wasn't for the last time that night. She wondered what the chances were that someone so much like her, so cute and so charming and so funny, could have randomly met her at work. If she had been in the back that day, or if Lania hadn't been so mean to him, or . . . it never would have happened. And while mentioning Xavier and his subsequent sickness with him was not the sort of thing one did on a first date (*or ever, really*), Chloe could definitely see talking to Brian about other things. Her mom, her dad, Paul and Ame, her near-death experience . . .

"Well, there they are," Brian said, indicating the big yellow cats.

Chloe put her hand out to the rail. She had always sort of dismissed lions before as the popular and inevitable members of any zoo tour. Common, even. But she looked at them more closely now. One female rose and walked languidly over to a water trough. Every step was casual; her shoulders moved up and down slowly. There was no mistaking the power in her muscles. Somehow Chloe wasn't surprised when, after taking a gentle lap and letting the droplets hang from the fur around her mouth, the lion turned and looked directly at her, golden eyes into her own hazel ones.

"I never realized how beautiful they were before," Chloe whispered, unable to turn away.

Brian was saying something, spilling off factoids

about the big cats, but she wasn't listening. She could feel her dream again, like it was real.

". . . know all about these guys. In the wild they eat like ten *pounds* of meat a day, sleep up to twenty *hours* a day, and can run up to fifty miles an hour. . . ."

You need a desert, Chloe thought at them. The lioness showed no sign of hearing or caring about her. She wandered back over to the other females and let herself down onto the ground, lazily and heavily. She bit at her paw.

"Uh, Chloe? Chloe?" Brian asked, waving his hand in front of her.

"What? Sorry?"

"I was trying to impress you with my *National Geographic*–like knowledge of the big cats."

"Oh, sorry. Very clever." Chloe turned for one last look at the lionesses. "These don't just kill people, like Siegfried and Roy's tiger?"

Brian snorted. "Lions aren't usually as dangerous as tigers. But they're not house cats, either. They can get annoyed or pissed off—and even the friendly ones, like these, don't know their own strength compared to humans. They can accidentally kill a zookeeper while trying to play with him."

"Oh." Chloe thought about that last fact, and Xavier.

"We should probably go; it closes in like ten minutes."

"Oh yeah. Of course." Chloe shook her head. "I have to get you your monkey!"

Brian smiled shyly. "You don't really have to. . . ."

93

"Of course I do, silly. This was a *great* idea for a date." She grinned.

"Date . . . ?" he asked, surprised. Chloe hit him playfully on the shoulder. As the twilight deepened and they headed back to the main entrance, Chloe felt a surge of energy jolt through her, making her skip, babble incessantly, and touch Brian as she talked, without embarrassment or reserve. She even bought him an extra-big monkey, one with long arms and Velcro so he could wear it around his neck.

They made it out just as the gates closed.

"This was great—thanks for suggesting it," Chloe said honestly. Her bus was coming; he was going in the opposite direction.

"Oh, cool. I'm glad you enjoyed it."

She waited. He seemed to be looking anxiously for the bus. "Can I see you again?" Chloe finally asked, a little annoyed that *she* had to be the one to bring it up. Hadn't she bought him a monkey, after all?

"Oh—yeah—of course. If you want." He looked down at her, unsure.

"Of course I do! Didn't I just say this was, like, the best date ever?" The bus stopped and opened its doors. "Aren't you going to kiss me?" Chloe asked, the first real flirty thing she had said all evening.

He leaned over and kissed her delicately on the cheek.

"Good night, Chloe," he said softly, and turned around and walked away.

Chloe climbed into the bus, feeling her cheek with her fingers, wondering if this was as close to a normal guy her age as she was ever going to date.

As soon as she was sure he wasn't looking, at the last moment she dove off. There were *other* ways to get home. She took off her jacket, tied it around her waist— and ran.

This time she concentrated on more and more outrageous leaps, sometimes running along a line of parked cars, bouncing from roof to roof. When she turned off the street and started running through tiny parks, fences proved no issue: she vaulted over short ones and leapt as high as she could onto chain-link ones, throwing herself over the top and jumping all the way to the ground, sometimes as far as twelve feet.

A pit bull strained on its leash in the courtyard of one run-down condo complex; a beautifully groomed old yellow Lab barked at her, nipping at her legs as she streaked by. Even Mrs. Languedoc's nasty little shih tzu howled like a wolf at her when Chloe finally ran up her own driveway.

"Kimmy, what's wrong with you?" Chloe heard her neighbor scold the dog.

Chloe wandered over to the cheap picket fence. This time she was breathing heavily, and her lower stomach was cramping—Chloe wondered how badly she would pay for this exercise session tomorrow. She stuck her hand between the plastic slats to let the dog nose her.

They had never been particularly good friends in the past, but Chloe had occasionally thrown it raw hot dogs, trying to get it to shut up when Mrs. Languedoc was away.

Kimmy growled, backed away to a safe distance, and began barking again.

"Whatever." Chloe shrugged and went inside.

"How was your study session?" her mother called from the table, where she was paying bills on her laptop.

It took Chloe a moment to remember exactly what lie she had told.

"Lousy. We got *nothing* done." She threw her jacket into the closet with disgust. "I just don't see why Lisa keeps inviting Keira along. All she wants to do is gossip and bitch."

"Well, if you need help"—Chloe's mom looked over at her and smiled—"I was great at trig."

Of course. You were freaking great at everything.

"Thanks." Chloe gave her a weak smile and went upstairs to the bathroom.

Blood.

On her boy panties, in the front part of the cotton crotch. Bright red. Her ten-dollar *nice* boy panties.

Her first thought was that she had ripped her hymen during one of the gigantic leaps off fences she had taken, legs spread wide.

Then as she felt more wetness on the inside of her leg, she realized what it was.

Holy shit. She finally got her period.

"About time," she muttered, and started rooting through the bathroom cabinet. That must have been what set the dogs off. They must have smelled the blood on her. She finally found a box of tampons—another thing that, if she didn't like her mother's brand, she would have to start paying for herself.

I have to call Amy, she thought. Chloe smiled.

And then she got a cramp.

Nine

"Hey—where were you last night?" Amy demanded. Once again, the bus had arrived early or someone at the school had arrived late, and they had to wait *outside* for the first bell. It was a brisk fall morning, and, like many other students, Chloe had not dressed for extended outside lounging; she stamped her feet and balled her fists into her pockets, considering bumming a cigarette.

"I had a date," Chloe responded coolly. It was easy in this temperature.

"With Alyec?"

"No. Someone else."

Amy regarded her for a long moment. She was going sort of mod today, sort of Austin Powers, in a big purple fake-fur coat and goggles.

"What the fuck, King?" she finally said. "First you don't even answer when I invite you to my poetry reading and now you announce this little secret life—"

Chloe knew how she *wished* she could respond. Like

the people on TV who always had a good answer, the proper words, just enough righteous indignation:

"*I* have a secret life? Since you and Paul started dating, it's like neither of you exist anymore. We haven't really seen each other except for my birthday, and suddenly you're pissed that I won't come to your poetry reading you so *graciously deigned* to invite me to?"

Or at least the heartfelt, emotionally genuine pre-mutual-crying speech:

"Amy, I've really felt abandoned recently. I know that you and Paul have suddenly become very important in each other's lives, and I respect that—but *we're* friends, too. A lot has been going on in my life I haven't had a chance to tell you about—and you're my best friend. I really need you sometimes, and lately I feel that you just haven't been there for me."

But, "I'll be at your poetry reading," was what she actually said, grudgingly, looking at the ground.

"Oh." Amy looked confused, then relieved. "Thanks. Maybe you'll tell me about your secret lover *then*?"

"Yeah. Whatever." There was a long pause. Chloe sensed that this was a crux of a moment, what could be the beginning of a serious rift. For a second it was breathtaking, like she was poised at the edge of a canyon, at the top of a tower, ready to jump: no more annoying, pretentious Amy *or* weirdness with Paul, just a slow parting of ways behind her. In front were Alyec or Brian, the new things she could suddenly seem to do, the freedom and excitement of the night.

But she wasn't ready for that yet. An image came to her mind of the lionesses in her dream and at the zoo. If they were human, they wouldn't even let something as small or foolish as this waste their time.

"Could you ask Paul to come a little later?" Chloe finally asked. "Give us some girl time to catch up?"

Amy's face softened.

"Yeah, of course! Totally. Come by at seven."

"Will do."

They were silent for a moment, awkward in their emotions.

"So . . . like my coat?" Amy finally asked.

"How many Muppets died to make that thing?" Chloe shot back, grinning.

Chloe was in a state of mental panic when Alyec called out to her in the hallway. She didn't hear him, overwhelmed by what she had just promised. Amie's poetry readings were something not to be believed.

Chloe thought madly about tiny FM radios that she could hide in her ear and pull her hair over to hide, about getting very badly drunk or stoned, about getting one of the loopier Wiccans at school to put her into a trance before the reading. *Anything* that could get her through it with her sanity intact and a straight face.

She and Paul used to sometimes have to hold hands during them, squeezing for strength and distraction during the bad parts, keeping the other restrained if she or Paul couldn't fight the urge to giggle or get up and run screaming from the café. Somehow she didn't think that would be happening with Paul *this* time, however.

Maybe I can puncture my eardrums....

"Hey! Chloe!"

She finally looked up and realized that Alyec had been waving to her and calling her name for a few minutes. He ran down the hall to catch up with her.

"Sorry." She shook her head. "Lost in thought."

"No problem." He looked her up and down. Suddenly Chloe was self-conscious about her second-day jeans and her Strokes T-shirt with the bleach hole. Even her undies were the last ones before the wash: nasty, unsexy thongs. "I tried IM-ing you last night, but you weren't on."

Me? You were IM-ing me, *you hunka hunka icebergy love?* He smiled at her, a little puzzled, a little expectantly. Chloe immediately began to come up with some non-ego-shattering lie she could tell him about why she wasn't around that would keep him calm and interested, that would cut the conversation short and move them on to pleasanter topics.

Then she noticed how close he was standing, very much in her space, looming over and looking down at her. Kind of obnoxious. Like she was the kind of girl who *enjoyed* being loomed over by the sexiest guy in her class in the middle of the hall.

"I had a date," she answered, shrugging.

"Like, a study date?"

She almost laughed at his quick assumption. "No, a *date* date." She turned and began walking to her next class.

"Wait, what?" He ran to catch up with her again. "Who?"

"Brian. You don't know him."

"Does he go to Mary Prep?"

A wicked gleam came into her eye. "No," she answered casually. "He's not in high school."

"King, you are one hell of a tease." He sighed.

"Tease?" She turned and faced him finally. "Uh, I don't see anyone else making demands on my time."

"*That* is definitely teasing," Alyec called after her when she walked away again. "If I understand English properly."

She waved *buh-bye* at him over her shoulder.

Reflecting on the encounter later, Chloe had to admit she was thrilled with the way Alyec had no inclination to keep their little tête-à-tête silent. He was obviously after her, loudly, in the middle of the hall and didn't seem to care if anyone—even Keira and her gang—heard him. The whole school now knew that Alyec Ilychovich wanted Chloe King.

It was a nice feeling and made her feel even cozier with the cold day outside and her inside the thick-wood-and-velvet café, hands wrapped around a hot cider. She snuggled back into her seat, pretending to not see the microphone and spotlight being set up in a corner.

"He-e-e-y!" Amy came in, looked around, waved to the people setting up, kiss-kissed them on their cheeks, and told them she would be with them in just a few minutes. Even though it was a little thing, Chloe was pleased that her friend cared enough to put off what was a fairly adoring crowd to spend time with her. Which did not stop Chloe from putting her hand up just in time to prevent Amy from air kissing her, too. There *were* limits. *The pretension ends here.*

"So . . . what? *What?* What are all these things happening in the life of Chloe King?" Amy turned and screamed, "I'll get a tea, over here, Earl Grey, with lemon!"

"Well, first things first." Chloe shifted back and forth uncomfortably. "What kind of tampons do you use?"

Amy's jaw dropped. "Oh my *God*. You finally got your *period*?"

Chloe winced, trying to draw her hair down over her face. She felt the tips of her cheeks, right under her eyes, go hot and pink.

"Tell the entire world," she mumbled.

"Oh. Uh, sorry. I'm just . . . amazed. And glad you're, like, normal and stuff. No weird tumors or something." Amy's eyes went glassy. "You're a woman! You've finally joined us in the cycle of life and—"

"Save the goddess shit for later. I'm uncomfortable and cramping."

"Try 'slenders.' You have to change them more often, but that's what I used until I started having sex. . . ." Her friend's face suddenly furrowed. "Jeez, you're going to have to start taking all that stuff seriously now. Maybe go on the pill. Condoms break, you know, and you could get pregnant—"

"Thanks for the sex-ed speech. I only needed the relevant part. 'Slenders.' I get it. Thanks." She looked at her cider and admitted, "Besides, it's not like I've even had actual intercourse yet . . . and it doesn't look like it's a possibility anytime in the near future."

"Yeah, Paul and I haven't had sex yet. Even if we were at that point, he's, you know, old-fashioned and stuff."

Chloe shuddered. Thinking of Paul having sex made her think of Paul having a penis, and Paul's penis was definitely something she never wanted to think about. Much less Amy *and* Paul having sex. Together.

"I know you two are serious, and I'm happy for you," Chloe said slowly, "but it would be nice if you kept some parts of it . . . to yourself, you know?"

Amy blinked. Her blue eyes made her look extra innocent. "Who else am I going to talk to about it?"

"You can *talk* to me about it," Chloe said, "but just censor the dirty parts, you know? This is *Paul*. And besides"—she came up with a brilliant excuse—"do you really think he would want *me* knowing these things about him? He gets all blushy about a trip to the *doctor*."

"I hadn't thought about that," Amy said after a long

moment. She fiddled with the hand charm on her necklace that had lost its silver tarnish long ago from other nervous musings. Chloe smiled; she remembered when her friend first got it, years ago, from her grandmother. . . .

"Well, what about *you*? What happened to Alyec?"

"Nothing. He's still on my 'watch' list." Chloe grinned like a very self-satisfied cat over the rim of her cup. "It's just that I met this other guy, Brian. He comes to Pateena now and then. Totally cute. He's working a couple of years before applying to college. I think you'd like him; he knits his own hats. He took me out for coffee last night." She didn't feel like telling her the part about the zoo; there was something strangely private about it. In a nice sort of way. Not meant for sharing, not even with Amy.

Hey, he never gave me the hat pattern, she realized.

A size-zero girl in all black brought over a mug of tea with slices of lemon on a saucer. Amy busied herself preparing the tea exactly as she liked it, and Chloe watched more people come in, filling the dark corners of the café like large, quiet rats.

"I think that fall affected you more than we thought," Amy finally said.

"What are you talking about?" Chloe said, a little offended by the cavalier way her friend spoke.

"Come on—*two* guys? One is the most popular in our class, the other not even in high school? You? *Chloe King?*" Amy shook her head. "That's not like you at all."

Good thing I didn't tell her about Xavier, Chloe decided.

106

But it gave her pause: Amy was right. It used to be that Chloe never would have gone after *any*one in the popular crowd, no matter how cute or nice. And a guy not at their high school? *Any* high school? Two years older than her? Old enough to vote and look at porn? *Fuggedaboutit!* And what exactly about going to a club by herself and picking up a stranger and making out with him in back?

Chloe looked at Amy's necklace again, suddenly brought back to the girl she was at Amy's party when they were both thirteen. A very different girl.

"I'm blooming," she answered with a hint of irony in her voice.

"Exploding, more like." She winced at Chloe's look. "In a *good* way," she quickly added. "What's Brian look like?"

"Tall, dark and brooding, handsome, brown eyes, mysterious smile . . . He didn't kiss me good night, though."

"Gay," Amy decided.

"I wasn't exactly getting a 'gay' vibe," Chloe said defensively.

"All right, maybe he's just shy."

"Hey." Chloe suddenly really *saw* her friend's necklace. It looked suspiciously like a cat, lying down, a smug little smile on her face. She furrowed her brow and reached for it.

"Don't you remember? Nana gave it to me when she came back from Egypt. For my bat mitzvah."

"Yeah, yeah. But what is it supposed to *be*, exactly?"

"Um . . . a cat goddess of some sort, I think." Amy pulled it out and tried to look at it. "Bastet or something? It was back when I was totally obsessed with cats, when I got Pharaoh." That was the original name of the all-black kitten she'd rescued from an alley. Now he was huge and fat and just called Kitty.

"Ma chérie!" a draggle-haired *Moulin Rouge* extra in a long white silk scarf called to Amy. "We await your presence."

"Yeah—give this to Paul when he comes, will you?" Amy fished a brown, letter-sized bag out of her giant denim one. "He left it at my place Wednesday night."

After her friend joined the other poetry weirdos, Chloe pulled the package closer to her so no one would take it or sit on it. *Left it at her place Wednesday night.* The three of them used to watch cheap DVD rentals at Amy's midweek when everything was getting too stressful, usually Bollywood musicals. She was the only one with a TV in her room. They would pop popcorn and watch gold and pink dancers twirl and sing and elephants march by and feel like they were at the edge of another world, somewhere far more interesting, beyond Inner Sunset. Chloe wondered what they watched last night, or if they just made out.

She opened Paul's package: comics. Wednesday was comic day, something he had drilled into her since they were nine.

She flipped through them—some starred recognizable characters like Batman and Green Lantern, others were just as brightly colored but with superheroes she had never heard of. Some were called things like *Hellblazer* and filled with amazingly disgusting scenes of people and demons doing extreme violence to each other. Chloe had learned a long time ago to avoid looking at those.

She pulled a couple out; there was at least another fifteen minutes before the readings began. *Batman* was familiar but way too short, and the ads were more intriguing than the plotline. She opened another one about a woman called Selina Kyle and followed the four-color panes through her adventures leaping and running across the Gotham City skyline. Chloe grinned, thinking of herself.

Then she frowned.

Is that it? Is that what I have? Superpowers?

She had never thought of it that way before. It sort of added up, though, if you looked at it from a comic book point of view: She'd survived a fall that should have killed her, she'd fought a guy—with no previous training—who was twice as big as her and used to living on the street, she could run for miles without getting winded and jump hurdles like a track star—when she used to have all the physicality of a slug. And here she'd been assuming that part of it was just some sort of growing spurt. . . .

"Hey, since when did *you* become a comic mooch?" Paul asked, sliding into the booth across from her.

"Since I was bored out of my mind." She showed him the comic book she was reading. "Do any of these guys have, like, more subtle powers? Besides flying?"

"Selina Kyle doesn't *have* powers," he said with a little bit of smugness. "Neither do Batman or Robin. John Constantine is . . . questionable. Aquaman can breathe underwater, which I guess is subtle, but he can also talk to fish. Why?"

"Just wondering." She watched as he carefully put the comics back in their Mylar bags and slid them gently into the brown bag. "So, how long is this horror scheduled to last?"

"An hour and a half."

Chloe groaned. The lights dimmed and people clapped politely. The man with the scarf gave a little introduction. Chloe almost wished she still had a comic to look at. The poets were theoretically in order of who signed up first, but they tended to let the least worst go last.

Which meant that Amy was usually second or third.

If I'm a superhero, Chloe idly thought, *I should definitely get some better clothes. Clingier. Spandex. Tank tops and bike shorts.* Where did superwomen keep their extra tampons, anyway? Her foot tapped; she tried to keep it quiet through the first few readings. She would have given almost anything to be able to run outside. She hoped one of the poets' clove cigarettes would fall and catch the place on fire.

"And now, Amy Scotkin, reading three of her works."

"Whoo-hoo!" Chloe shouted, cupping her hands to her mouth like she was at a sporting event.

"Go, Amy!" Paul shouted.

Amy blushed. "My first one, 'Night Swan.'"

"Holy crap," Chloe whispered in horror. "She's doing the 'Swan' again? All thirteen verses?"

"Hey, a little support and positive thought might be welcome here," Paul suggested.

> Lo, my lover lies asleep
> In a twin bed with black satin sheets
> In the gable nook of our hallowed nest. . . .

Chloe clenched and unclenched her hands the entire time, her fingernails tingling. She looked over at Paul; he sat still—*trying* to look serious, she thought.

> Call, call! *My night black swan!*
> *Weep for the love that is lost*
> *The scarlet threads of shame and shadow*
> *That flow betwixt my breasts* . . .

Thirteen verses and approximately fifteen minutes later it was over. There were still two more Amy "specials," but the last one was new, so at least it was an unexpected horror. And there was a break just two poets later.

"Holy shit," Chloe said as she and Paul went up to the bar afterward to reorder. "I think it gets harder every time."

"Yeah, some of those poets were atrocious," he agreed.

"And what about her new masterpiece? What gothic shit was she listening to when she wrote 'Daylight Incubus'?"

"You didn't like it?"

Chloe turned to stare at her friend. "Um—hello? It *sucked*, Paul."

"I don't think it was that bad," Paul demurred.

"If you mean that it wasn't any better or worse than any of the other stuff she's done, I agree."

"Why did you bother coming if you're just going to trash her?"

He didn't say it nastily—it wasn't a challenge. It almost sounded like a genuine question.

"Because that's what we always do, Paul!" Chloe said, exasperated. "We keep on trying to get her to drop this shit and do the stuff she's good at, she ignores us, we keep coming here to support her, she reads her poetry, and we—well, commiserate."

"She's my *girl*friend, now, Chlo," Paul said softly. Like it was supposed to shock her.

And it did.

"That doesn't change everything. Or at least it's not supposed to." Chloe spun on her heels and walked away, ignoring the tea that was set in front of her. *Has everyone gone insane?* It seemed like she was just getting back into sync with Amy, and Paul suddenly went off the deep end, taking this whole girlfriend-boyfriend thing way too seriously. He had always been a harder person to get to know than Amy, sometimes difficult to read, but these dreadful readings used to be their bonding time. He used to relax.

"Hey, good job," she said, kissing Amy on the cheek. "I gotta take off."

"Oh! Thanks!" Amy grinned. "See you tomorrow!"

Chloe stormed out into the cold, hands balled up into fists in her pockets again. She didn't feel like running; she felt an almost uncontrollable rage. Paul had always been kind of secretive and weird about his girlfriends before—but this was beyond beyond. His and Amy's relationship was the worst thing that had happened to the three of them.

And it's kind of your fault: they got together 'cause of the fall.

Chloe sighed, some of the steam going out of her. She unclenched her hands and realized she had been clutching a crumpled-up piece of paper in her pocket. She pulled it out and read it under a streetlight, assuming it was a permission slip or note or something. Her eyes widened when she realized what it actually said.

Chloe:
Your life is in danger. Be wary of the company you keep. Be prepared—and ready to run. The Order of the Tenth Blade knows who you are. . . .

A friend

113

Ten

Normal people called the police. That was what normal people did in situations like this with weird notes and death threats and things like that.

Too bad I'm not normal.

It was probably just a joke. Right? Chloe had been terrified in fourth grade when she found a note in her cubby telling her that she'd better "watch out." And that had turned out to be Laura Midlen's idea of funny. But somehow this seemed less amusing than that incident.

My life is in danger? Did that mean someone found out about Xavier? Maybe he was after her? That didn't make sense, though: she hadn't meant to hurt him, and it wasn't worth killing her over. What was the company she kept? Paul? Amy? Nothing strange about them or dangerous . . . Whoever wrote the note probably meant her new friends: either Alyec or Brian. More likely Brian since Alyec was a known factor, a normal high school kid with roots in the community. She didn't really know anything about Brian besides what he had told her. . . .

Then again, he could also be the "friend" who was warning her. But he hadn't been in the café—in fact, Chloe didn't really know anyone at the Black Rooster except by sight. When was the note slipped into her pocket? Maybe it wasn't even meant for her.

She checked the locks on the doors several times before going to sleep—or *trying* to go to sleep. She felt pretty sure she could handle a daytime attack by a street thug, but a nighttime ambush would be another story.

The next Monday at school Chloe was even grumpier and sleepier than usual. She kept looking up suddenly, jumping at noises, and seeing things out of the corners of her eyes. All for what was probably just a prank. As soon as she got a free period, she went to the newspaper office.

"Hey, Paul," she said, making straight for the couch.

"Chloe," he answered uneasily. He was sitting at the computer, playing some bright-colored and contraband video game.

"I'm wiped. Do you mind?" She threw herself into the couch.

"No. Go ahead." He stood up and played with a pencil for a minute. "I . . . might have overreacted Friday night. . . . Are we cool?" he finally asked.

Even through her sleep-thick haze, Chloe smiled. Paul actually cared if she was angry at him! Then again, she had a complete right to be.

She raised her arm to give him a thumbs-up.

"Cool." He threw his bag over his shoulder. "Just close the door on your way out, okay? It's already locked."

But Chloe was already asleep.

She woke up perfectly, precisely forty-five minutes later, *almost* in time for phys ed. Which was really odd because usually once Chloe was out, she was *flat* out until someone woke her up. The second, warning bell rang and dozens of classroom doors slammed shut, students trapped inside, being forced to learn.

She stretched and yawned and scratched herself, rolling her head and shaking the stiffness out of her shoulders—she hadn't moved from the position she'd fallen down in, and it wasn't really the most comfortable of couches.

She slumped out of the room, pausing to pick up the obituary sections of the local newspapers lying around and remembering to make sure the door was closed like Paul had said. She started down the hall toward gym, possibly her most-hated class. *Although,* she considered, *maybe I could surprise them with a thing or two.* But probably not. The one thing every TV show, book, and comic book had ever suggested about people with special powers was to never reveal them to the outside world. At the worst she could be kidnapped and dissected by the government. At best Mr. Parmalee would insist she go for a drug test.

"Chloe King!"

117

Alyec was coming down the empty hall. She smiled.

"What are *you* doing at this end of the school?"

"I am going for my flute lesson," he said, somewhat embarrassed. He held up a small black case. "I have always wanted to learn it, but there was no money or opportunity in Russia."

"Funny, I would have picked you for a boner," she said.

His eyes widened.

"*Trom*boner? You know? That and trumpet are what all of the popular guys play."

"Well, I am not a normal popular guy. And anyway, if I am so popular, how come you haven't asked to see me since the sea lions?" There was a sexy little smile that he was just hiding. Chloe felt a shiver run through her body. "How's *Brian*?"

"He's great." *Except for that whole lack-of-kissing-and-phone-calls thing.*

"Oh yeah? You really like him, huh? *I* think you're just playing hard to get."

"Awww, what's the matter? Keira not enough for you?"

"Nope," he answered, grinning. Then he leaned over and kissed her. "She is just a stupid little girl," he whispered into her ear, brushing it with his lips.

Although such things had been placed far, far from her mind since—well, since her period began, Chloe felt the desire she had felt with Xavier rise up through her

118

again. She turned her head so they were cheek to cheek, her lips against his jaw.

"We should go somewhere," he whispered, kissing the tops of her cheeks over and over again.

"Janitor's closet," Chloe breathed, pointing.

They both broke for it. Unlike on TV, this one was filled with actual janitorial stuff—mops and buckets and bottles of cleanser—and there was no real room to stand. They looked at it, then at each other.

Chloe giggled. Unlike the time with Xavier, this was playful and fun. Alyec threw himself against the back of the closet so he would bear the brunt of their weight and pulled her in after him as she closed the door.

Everything was very close and warm. She could smell all the disparate aspects of Alyec: his cologne, the fabric softener on his clothes, his toothpaste, the shampoo or gel in his hair, his skin and his breath.

Also Lysol and Mr. Clean, but she tried not to think about that.

He put his hands around her face and kissed her full on the lips, the way she had been aching for Brian to do the other night. He didn't stop, not even to breathe, feeling every corner and surface of her mouth with his own.

The way a girl should *be kissed,* was Chloe's last coherent thought.

When they stumbled out into the bright light of the hallway later, it was, fortunately, still empty. Alyec had to clap his hand over her mouth once or twice when they were in the closet because she was giggling and making him giggle, too. But no one had come by. She pulled and adjusted her shirt.

"You are one sexy girl, Chloe King," Alyec said, kissing her one last time on the cheek. "That was powerful stuff in there."

She *felt* pretty sexy. But . . .

"Well, and now you can tell all your friends that. How you finally cornered Chloe King and you had the time of your life." She smiled weakly.

Alyec frowned. "Do you really think I'm like that? Chloe, I was serious about Keira. She means *nothing* to me. And I'm *not* a complete dick."

Chloe nodded. She hoped, of course. In nice-guy competitions Brian had him definitely beat. She reshouldered her bag and then realized Alyec was empty-handed.

"Where's your flute?" she asked.

They looked back into the closet and saw the black case sticking out of a bucket.

Getting out of gym was easy—as soon as she and Alyec parted, she ran for the nurse's office and made a big deal about how she was *bleeding* and this was her *first period ever* and she was cramping and had spent the whole time in the bathroom. The nurse was brusquely sympathetic and promised to speak to Mr. Parmalee before it was officially filed as a cut. She also recommended that Chloe get her gyn exam ASAP. Chloe agreed and left, limping a little as if she was still in pain.

She had texted Amy earlier about meeting for lunch—in the corner of the cafeteria near the pay phones. It wasn't a desirable area, but at least they would be left alone. She planned on showing her the note. Maybe even telling her the truth about . . . *Well, about what?* Running really fast? Kissing Alyec in the closet? Whatever. Anyway, Amy loved mysteries—she had gone through a whole *Harriet the Spy*/*Nancy Drew*/Agatha Christie stage that had lasted a lot longer than those of most little boys and girls who were interested in being detectives. Even if she had no idea what to make of the note, at least it would be entertaining. After all, maybe the note wasn't even meant for her. Maybe it was a mistake.

Chloe looked up and around the cafeteria, then at her watch. They only had twenty minutes for lunch today, and five of them were already gone. Amy hadn't texted her back, but that didn't mean anything. One of them always said "meet me here" and the other one just showed up. It had always been like that. Unless there was a problem—that was the only reason for a response, if one of them couldn't make it.

She checked her phone. No messages.

At 12:35 she finally gave up, realizing Amy wasn't going to show.

•   •   •

121

She had the whole evening to herself, sort of a nice change from recent events. And sort of not. Chloe did some desultory straightening of her room and read a little of *The Scarlet Letter* for class. She went to the computer and surfed for a while, downloading MP3s and seeing what her favorite celebrities were up to. Then on a whim she searched on AIM for Alyec Ilychovich . . . and there he was. Under Alyec Ilychovich. *He sure does have a lot to learn about hiding your real identity and other American things.* Chloe smiled and added him to her buddy list. His account was private—*such a popular guy!*—so she sent him an invite from oldclothesKing, one of her more common aliases. Then she went on surfing.

There was an e-mail from Brian on her Hotmail account:

> Chloe,
> I really enjoyed our playdate the other night. But I never gave you the pattern!
> Do you like ska? Downtime hosts Kabaret Saturdays, no cover. No penguins, but it should be a cool night otherwise. If not, maybe you have an idea . . . ?
> —Brian 415-555-0554

She smiled. He was just so . . . perfect. It was almost like he could sense she was lonely and sent this. She called him but got his answering machine.

"Hi, this is Whit Rezza—if you're looking for Peter

Rezza, you can reach him on his cell, 415-555-1412. Leave a message, thanks!"

"Hey, Brian, it's Chloe. I'd *love* to go out on Saturday—not a huge fan of ska, but I like it enough. Just going to have to figure out what to tell my mom first; she's not big on me and guys. So this is a possible 'yes,' and . . ."

The electronic sound of a door opening came from her computer. She looked over; Alyec was online. A second later there was a *beep* as he accepted her invite.

"And I'll call you or e-mail you later, okay? Bye!"

She would have to remember to call before her mom came home; on the home phone bill it would only appear as a local call, but on her cell phone the bill listed every number. And her mom went through the bill *very* carefully each month, demanding to know what unrecognizable phone numbers were. She said it was for budget reasons . . . *ha!*

Chloe spun back in her chair so she was facing the computer. There was already a message from Alyec.

Alyec: Miss me yet?

She giggled.

Chloe: Only your lips. The rest of you—well, whatever.
Alyec: Shallow girl! I have a brain, too, you know.
Chloe: Yeah?
Alyec: And more . . .

Chloe flushed. She had felt a lot of his body—fully clothed—in the closet. She wished it was summer so they could go to the beach and she could rub oil all over his broad shoulders. Or that they could date like normal people. *Too bad I'm not normal,* she thought for the second time in a week.

The phone rang.

Chloe: Hang on, brb.

"King residence," she answered.

"Hey—uh—Chloe—was that you who called?" Brian's voice came from the other end. "My dad has caller ID and callback on this thing."

"Yeah, it was me." She was still flushed, thinking about Alyec and his body and the closet, and suddenly found herself thinking about Brian. More specifically, her on top of Brian, holding him down while she kissed him. *I'll bet I could do that with my new strength, too. . . .*

He must have heard something funny in her voice.

"Are you okay?"

"Yeah, I'm fine. Why?"

"Oh. You just sounded—never mind. So, you still want that pattern?"

No, I want you, *you dillhole.*

There was a beep from the computer:

Alyec: I'm waiting. . . .

124

Or Alyec. I want Alyec, too. It was funny right this moment, the two guys on two different means of communication. But soon, if her life was anything like TV— or even real life—it would all get very complicated without a decision. *But not yet. Not just yet!*

"Yeah. Should we try for Saturday?"

"Uh, sure. That's fine. I mean, it's great!" There was a long pause. "Chloe? I, uh . . ."

"Yeah?" She waited to hear him say that she was too young for him, that they had to break up, that he didn't find her attractive. She sucked in her breath. *So much for me making a decision.*

"Uh, nothing. I just think you're cool, that's all."

"Oh." She grinned. "Thanks."

"Yeah, so call me about Saturday, okay?"

"Absolutely."

There was another beep from the computer.

Alyec: Chloe King is so full of herself that she lets Alyec Ilychovich, one of the most popular guys in class, hang on the telephone. Or computer. Or whatever.

"All right, then, bye."

He hung up sounding excited, pleased, and embarrassed. Chloe ran back to the keyboard.

Alyec: Doopy doo, doopy doopy doo . . .
Chloe: *All right, all right!* Jeez, can't a girl pee?

Alyec: I'll bet you were talking with your other boyfriend.

Chloe froze. Now would be a good time to say something.

Chloe: If by talking you mean urinating and boyfriend you mean toilet, then yes.

Alyec: Your sexy talk is leaving me all hot.

Chloe: Ewww! I didn't know you were into stuff like that.

Alyec: Hey, we foreign boys are weird.

Chloe: At least you have nice lips.

Alyec: Oh, and you don't even know the half of what they can do.

Chloe: Yeah? Want to give me a hint?

Alyec: I can blow up balloons really fast.

Chloe: Now who's being the tease?

Alyec: Why? What do you want me to do with my lips?

They typed back and forth furiously for several hours, taking breaks to go get drinks, or more bathroom breaks, or to IM other people. Alyec told her that Jean Mehala was just asking him if he had any desire to join the Junior UN. *I am the junior UN!* And Lotetia wanted him on the dance committee, which he might just do; most of the music at the dances sucked.

Chloe: It must be neat being so wanted.

Alyec: Yeah? And exactly how do you want to be wanted?

There was a noise behind Chloe, the slightest scratch of a throat. She jumped and spun around, expecting a murderer or something awful.

It was worse. It was her mom.

"Who is that you're talking to?" Mrs. King demanded. She was wearing her driving glasses and looked stern and real mommish for once. Her gray eyes narrowed, and she gripped her attaché like an ax.

"How long were you standing there?" Chloe demanded.

"What was it you two *did* at school today that was so exciting?" From the set of her lips it was obvious that she had a pretty good idea already. She must have been standing there for quite a while. How had Chloe not heard her?

"Nothing," Chloe said dully.

"Making out in a *janitor's closet?* During *class?*"

"It was only gym. And besides—it's not like you let me go out on actual *dates.*"

"This is precisely why!" Her mother hit the computer screen violently enough to make it ring. "You are *grounded,* young lady! For the next week at least!"

"That's so unfair!" Normally Chloe would have been thinking about how badly she'd screwed up right then and doing whatever she could to make up for it—lie, apologize, finish out the normal teenage fight, and act good for the next week—but real anger was growing inside her, and she found she couldn't think. "Everyone else *dates*—and I have to lie and sneak around, even with *nice* guys like Brian. . . ."

"Who's *Brian*?" her mother demanded. Her hands shook with rage.

"What does it matter? He's totally great, but you won't let me date *him*, either!"

"It seems like you're doing well enough, whoring around like—" She fell silent.

Chloe just looked at her, eyes like coals. She couldn't hear; rushes of blood and fury rose in her. For the first time since she was a child, she had the almost overwhelming urge to hit her mother.

"Take. That. Back."

Mrs. King bit her lip.

"I'm—sorry. I didn't mean—that was way too harsh. I apologize. I shouldn't speak to you like that." She played with the hammered silver earring on her left ear, tugging at it.

"You're going to give me the whole 'how hard it is to be a single mom' speech now, aren't you?" Chloe spat.

"No, I—"

"Are you going to 'keep me' from dating when I'm in college? Jesus Christ, Mom, I'm *sixteen*. I have a job. I get good grades. What psycho-pop book did you get this 'no dating' bullshit out of?"

"It wasn't a book!" Mrs. King said, her voice rising again. Then she fell back on her heels, suddenly tired, all energy and anger drained from her face. "It was the last thing your father said before he disappeared. He made me promise to never let you date."

Chloe's jaw dropped, but she had nothing to say. The man she had been glorifying and missing for twelve years was the one responsible for this?

"This is *bullshit*," Chloe growled. She spun on her heels and pushed past her mother.

"Chloe, wait—"

She ran into the bathroom and slammed the door.

"FUCK!" she screamed. She clenched her fists, fingers aching painfully. She pulled back to punch the door.

And then she stopped.

There were claws where her nails had been. White and sharp and curved and beautiful, just like a cat's.

Eleven

She sat on the top of a chain-link fence, staring at the moon.

It was easy now, sitting like that on the balls of her feet with her hands just touching the rail. Now that she *knew* she was different.

"He made me promise to never let you date. . . ."

Why? Did he know something? Did it have to do with the claws?

Chloe lifted one hand and looked at it, trying to will them back. She bent her knuckles. She tried to remember the rage she'd felt. *What was it that she said that set me off?*

"Whoring around like—"

Sslt.

With the slightest of noises, the claws came out. They seemed to spring right from the bone, strong and sturdy as an extension of her hand. They didn't bend when she touched them, and the tips were razor sharp.

Xavier.

Maybe she'd scratched him with the tips. Maybe they were poisoned. Maybe they came out when she was all hot as well as enraged. *Is that why Dad didn't want me to date? Because I can accidentally kill people?*

She thought about what Brian had said at the zoo.

"Even the friendly ones . . . don't know their own strength compared to humans. They can accidentally kill a zookeeper while trying to play with him. . . ."

What if she had been face-to-face with her mom when she got that angry? Would she have lost control and tried to hit her? Would the claws have come out, scarring or killing her mother?

Suddenly her new powers didn't feel like fun anymore. They felt lethal.

So I can't make out with guys? But Alyec was fine. . . . It didn't make any sense.

A thousand mysteries, none of which were easily solved. Chloe felt an incredible surge of loneliness envelop her. Who could she talk to? Who could help her? Who would tell her that everything would be okay?

How can I even have a boyfriend?

Either he'd have to be *awfully* accepting and tight-lipped, or she would have to constantly hide things from him.

She stood up on the fence with ease: the trick was not to think about what she was doing and let her body just do it, she discovered. The roof of a nearby apartment complex hung just within reach. She leapt.

The sheer power in her body was phenomenal—as her legs flexed, she felt the way racehorses looked, all muscle and speed, no wasted movement or flesh. Her powerful thighs arced her easily over the gutter.

Landing was a little harder.

Chloe pitched forward, forgetting to compensate for momentum. She threw her arm out and managed to grab the base of an old antenna to keep herself from rolling off the roof. She lay against the tar tiles a moment, panting, scared to move, her feet dangling down. When she finally calmed down enough to think straight, she swung her left leg up and, bending her knee so she looked like a frog, pushed herself up onto the apex of the roof and swung her right leg over the other side so that she straddled it.

Not quite perfect.

Above her the stars glittered coldly in the dark blue sky. She looked out over the other roofs, the strange landscape with shingles and tiles for grass and chimneys and antennae for bushes and trees. Like the canopy layer in a rain forest, it was a whole area of the world she had never really noticed before. *Not before Coit Tower, at least.* And now it lay open to her. Some of the chimneys really were organic looking, like that kind of lumpy one—

Which was waving to her.

She stared harder. Chloe'd had better-than-perfect vision from birth, but, as on the night with the mugger, she realized she could see things far more clearly under the dim moonlight and night sky than she really should.

She waited and everything lightened, like in the viewfinder of a digital camera. She could see individual bricks and the mortar separating them.

The "chimney" elongated and straightened as the person stood up—balancing perfectly on the short wall that divided the roof space of one apartment building from the next. Then it crouched down, like a frog—*or a cat*—and leapt over the gap to the next building, landing so his—by the silhouette it looked more like a "his"— right hand came down onto the roof at the same time as his feet, ending in the same sort of crouch.

Oh, that's what I should have done, Chloe thought idly. *Spread my weight out across my legs* and *my hands so that . . .*

Then she realized.

This was him. The person from the note. *A friend.*

He was crouched very much like a cat on its haunches, arms and hands between his legs, watching her. He must be wearing all black, and his face was always in the shadows. He held up a hand—*paw*. What she was waiting for?

Chloe looked around. There was another house next to the one she was on, about ten feet away. An ugly, modern ranch like her own, with a tar roof. She started for it and then paused, scared. She looked up: he was still watching her. She took a deep breath and ran.

At the last moment she leapt, and instead of straight up like a high jumper, she stretched her body out almost like in a dive. She saw grass, sidewalk, and shadows pass far too quickly beneath her. Then her right hand touched the roof and her feet followed, landing in a perfect crouch.

Chloe had been holding her breath. She let it out and realized she was . . . *thrilled*. It was like the best free-fall ride at the park, no machinery necessary. Just her. She turned to look at the shadow figure across the street.

He gave her a thumbs-up, cocking his head. Then he leapt down off the roof on the other side, disappearing from sight.

"No!" Chloe cried, and looked around desperately for some quick way to get there, but there were no buildings that overhung the street or trees she could use to cross. She leapt down to the ground—without thinking this time; it was like she just decided to *fall*—and slipped down alongside the wall, landing with no sound. Her hands came flat against the pebbly concrete.

She ran across the street to the other side of the building. A single streetlight dimly illuminated an empty parking lot, gated shut. Someone had sprayed a colorful, huge tag on the brick wall that enclosed the far end. A plastic bottle rolled across the asphalt, pushed by an invisible breeze. Other than that and a billboard advertising Hankook Tires, nothing else was there.

What am I supposed to do now? For a few minutes it had looked like she had some strange sort of friend who could do the same things she could—and more. Who might be able to tell her who she was, why they were like this. What it all meant . . .

Ssst.

There was the faintest scratching noise above her. Chloe looked up and saw him crouching on top of a pole that supported a wire for the Muni electric buses. *I could have gotten across the street that way without coming down—but isn't it dangerous?*

As if to answer her question, he stood up and very carefully leapt onto one of the wires so that he never straddled the pole *and* it at the same time. Then he crouched down and sort of scuttled across it, using hands *and* feet to cling. He leapt up to the top of the billboard.

"How am I supposed to *get* up there?"

He jumped off the billboard, letting himself fall down its face. Ten neat rips in the paper lengthened as he fell, revealing the older ads underneath.

He had used his claws, she realized.

She walked over to the closest wood pole and tried swatting it. Nothing happened. She looked back at the shadow man and he crossed his arms impatiently. *Remember the jump,* she told herself. *No thought. Just do.* She leapt up and found herself clinging. Just with her hands and claws. *I'm gonna have the biggest delts,* she thought smugly. When she lifted her right hand for a grip farther up, her left hand and arm continued to supporting her; her claws were anchored deeply in the wood.

136

She quickly scuttled up the pole, using her legs at the last moment to vault herself up over the wires and onto the top. Chloe found herself grinning uncontrollably. The freedom of movement she now had—she could go anywhere—*anywhere*! Roofs, cliffs, tunnels, trees—all of those places outside normal human occupation. She could hide forever if she wanted or run across the skyline under stars, outside convention. *Free.*

She ran across the wire the way the shadow figure had but much faster and leapt to the billboard to meet him. But as soon as she landed, he took off for the gate, making an amazing leap to balance on its top bar.

"Hey!" she cried, laughing. A strange smell lingered behind him. He smelled like gasoline—like he'd fallen in a puddle of it. *An easy scent to follow.*

She tried to do the same as he did but wound up not quite making his last leap, falling into the parking lot, trapped—if, that is, she had been a normal human. She clambered up the gate and vaulted over it.

I could be a cat *burglar now.*

He was waiting for her, perched on a mailbox. But as soon as she recovered her breath, he was off again, running and leaping onto a fire escape, then climbing up to the roof.

Oh, you want to play, do you?

Chloe took off after him.

She chased him from rooftop to rooftop, from tree to telephone pole, neither of them ever touching the ground until they reached the park. Normally Chloe would never have even considered entering Golden Gate after dark—but obviously she was no longer a normal person. *Besides, he'll protect me if something happens.* Chloe felt sure of it.

It was mostly empty. Starlight wasn't enough to illuminate the paths, trees, and shadows, but her new night vision made everything, even the blackest dirt in the deepest shadow, glow like it was bathed in moonlight. The sidewalk gleamed like a fairy-tale road. She took to the grass instead, which was a little crunchy from the cold.

He paused near a bench under a ginkgo tree. He put his hands down as if to leap over it but instead straightened out so he was doing a handstand and then slowly let himself down the other way. *My arms aren't that strong,* was her first thought, before she realized what she had done that night already. He hooked his feet around a low branch and then pulled himself up into the tree.

Chloe ran forward, grabbed the top of the bench, and pushed, fully expecting to flip over and smash her face, arms, and body on the bench. But she straightened her hips when they were over her head and found herself doing a handstand as easily as if she had been a circus performer.

Suddenly there was a thud as all the weight in the world landed on her feet, bending and crushing her knees almost to her chin. And just as suddenly it was gone. Chloe lost her balance and tipped over onto the ground.

When she got up, she heard soft laughter, the first

noise he had made. He stood with his arms crossed several yards away: he had leapt down from the tree and used her feet and legs as a springboard.

"Funny," she said aloud.

He turned and ran again.

Chloe followed, straight into the trees and bushes, which had probably hidden a thousand muggers and rapists over the years. He darted from shadow to shadow, sometimes up a tree, sometimes over a shrub, always just keeping out of her reach. His scent was fading; if she lost sight of him, it would be over.

Suddenly she was at the other side of the park, in front of the exit. He was nowhere to be seen, and the scent trail was gone.

Chloe looked around, up trees and down the sidewalks, to see if he was hiding somewhere, waiting for her, ready to push her on again. But after five minutes there was still no sign.

"Come on," she called out plaintively. *"Please."*

With the excitement and the thrill of the hunt over, she suddenly felt lost. Just plain old Chloe King again, alone.

She started back the way she came, the shortest path through the park toward home, disappointed and sad.

Then she saw the oak tree.

About five feet up, its bark had been ripped to shreds by something with large claws, violently and deeply.

And under it, carefully dug in by single claw, was a smiley face.

Twelve

When Mrs. Abercrombie handed their quizzes back, Chloe had to remind herself: *Super-cat powers don't include the ability to do trig.* There was a big, ugly red D at the top of the page. Part of her fiercely didn't care; her life involved other things right now, more important things, like nighttime games of hide-and-seek and the fact that she wasn't like anyone else in class. Things like finding out about her past and what really happened to her dad.

But claws or no, Chloe was still Chloe, and she mentally calculated how much better she would have to do for the rest of the marking period to bring her grade back up to a respectable B. She snuck a glance over at Paul's paper and felt an evil satisfaction. He'd actually *studied* and only got a C.

When the bell rang, she got up and left quickly, giving Paul a quick "hey" in passing—but he was already making a beeline for Amy, who was out in the hall, waiting. Fortunately Alyec was also there, waiting for Chloe.

"Hey, Mamacita," he said. "How *you* doing?" The Spanish meets Joey from *Friends* spoken with a faint Russian accent was ridiculous, but his sexy face made it hard to take anything he said seriously, anyway.

"Hey." Unlike most other high school couples—note Amy and Paul—Chloe and Alyec did not kiss each other hello after class. They weren't even really a "couple"—which somehow made things sexier. They stood close without touching, faces inches apart.

"Do you want to go off campus for lunch, maybe?" he suggested. Chloe considered; this was strictly a no-no, grounds for detention, but it *was* a beautiful day out. *Just the sort for a picnic with a handsome Russian student.* She pictured them on a hillside under a tree with a Red Delicious or two, somewhere between the Garden of Eden and something more wholesome, like apple picking. *Too bad there's no place like that around here.*

"Absolutely," she said, deciding that McDonald's would have to do.

This was the closest thing to a date she and Alyec had ever really had, Chloe realized. Their relationship was sort of reversed. And this was no relaxing, bucolic hillside: just a bench outside the McDonald's, and the air was redolent of *fry*. At least it was a nice day.

"So . . . what was it like growing up in Russia?"

Alyec shrugged. He was very carefully arranging his cheeseburger, opening its wrapper and folding it around the

142

sandwich so that his fingers never touched it. Once it was properly (and somewhat daintily, Chloe thought) assembled, however, he opened his mouth wide and shoved in as much as he possibly could, like a normal teenager.

"The McDonalds there suck," he said, through a mouthful of meat. "They don't know how to do fries." Then he paused, reflecting. "Shakes were better, though."

"I'm *serious*, Alyec!"

"I *am* serious. They really are better. Not just McDonald's milk shakes, though. All ice cream and dairy."

"Yeah . . . ? And . . . ?" Chloe prompted him.

"And? It sucked. Nobody has any money, except New Russians. That's the mob. Everybody else—well, a movie costs a month's salary for most people. And a month's salary for many is like fifty dollars. A lot of people don't eat meat every day. So people drink a lot, you know?" His eyes narrowed, and for just a second Chloe thought she saw something deeper in them, something sad. But the moment was over and he shook his head. "At young ages, people start. I'll bet I could drink those football idiots under the table. But I don't," he added importantly.

Alyec poised over his remaining burgers and fries, deciding what to attack next.

Chloe dipped a single french fry into ketchup and chewed it slowly.

"How ever do you keep your girlish figure?" she asked.

"Sex," he answered promptly, setting about preparing another burger. In between he picked up a few fries *with*

143

a napkin—and bit off their heads. Then he popped the remainder into his mouth. All without touching them. Chloe was tempted to ask if this was a Russian thing or if he just had obsessive-compulsive disorder. "No, I am just kidding. I do eat a lot, though."

"What was St. Petersburg like?"

"Ha—Leningrad? Well, it is a beautiful city, for Russian cities at least, not like San Francisco, of course." He threw up his arm as if indicating the most obvious beauty in the world, but she didn't know if he meant the sky, the fog, the bridge, the weather, or what. "Lots of domes and steeples. Gold now because of restoration work. In the summer it is light until two o'clock in the morning, and the sun is low the entire time, very pretty. But really, it sucks."

She couldn't tell if he was embarrassed about his past, secretive, or just honest: that was his old life, but now it was over.

"I thought it was hard to emigrate," she said, trying to draw him out.

"*I* got a rich uncle."

"Is he a . . . New Russian?"

"Yeah, kind of like that." He looked sadly at the empty wrappers and plates.

"Teach me some Russian," she said, lying down and looking up at him.

"*Pazhoust,*" he said, leaning forward, his nose almost touching hers.

"What does that mean?" she whispered.

"'Please,'" he said, kissing her.

I should do that every *day,* thought Chloe as she waited for her bus home. While Alyec had not revealed himself to be a great thinker or philosopher or—er—someone with a sexy, mysterious, tortured past—he *was* an excellent kisser. The rest of the school day had passed in a dream—colors really did seem brighter and the future more optimistic.

And then Amy appeared.

"Want to hang tonight?"

Chloe took a moment to surface after she was torn rudely from her daydreams.

"Uh, what? No thanks. I really have to work on my trig. I'm in the danger zone," Chloe said coldly.

Amy stared at her a long moment, like a museum specimen she was trying to analyze. "What's your problem lately?"

"*My* problem?" Chloe felt an itchiness at her fingertips as her temper rose; she shrugged and twiddled her hands until it went away. *Clawing my friend's face off.* That's *a good way to end a fight. Especially with the whole school watching.* "What about *yesterday*? When I texted you about lunch and you totally blew me off?"

"I never got your message," Amy promptly denied. But there was a tiny hint of doubt in her voice.

"Check your mail," Chloe goaded. "Come on. Check it."

Making every movement flamboyant and impatient like she didn't have time for this sort of nonsense, Amy dramatically pulled out her phone and hit the buttons. "You see? There's no—*oh*." Her face fell. "That."

"'That'? So you *did* get it!"

"I was going to get back to you," Amy said carelessly. "Paul and I were busy. We were—"

"'Paul and I were busy'? What were you doing? Working on the newspaper or—hm, let me think—sucking face?"

"You—"

"'You and Paul' are *always* doing something. It's like the two of you are one unit and you've totally forgotten everything else."

"*Oh,* so that's it," Amy said, nodding. "You're jealous and lonely—is that why you're whoring around with dumbasses like Alyec?"

There was that word again. *Sheesh, one of my "boyfriends" won't even kiss me.* Chloe opened her mouth to *really* let Amy have it.

But as she thought about the other aspects of her life— her claws, her mysterious nighttime friend, Brian—she realized how ridiculous this argument was. There were a lot more important things going on, and Amy had as good as abandoned her the day of her fall. This was *not* worth it.

"Whatever. There's my bus." She turned and walked away, leaving Amy openmouthed and speechless.

• • •

She had to talk to someone about it.

Chloe had repeatedly backed down from arguments for the sake of their friendship—and Amy still treated her like the bad guy. She couldn't even see how she was acting! *I'd love to tell you what's going on in my life,* Chloe thought bitterly, *but you really don't seem that interested.*

Alyec would probably tell her to shrug it off, that it wasn't important. She wanted to bitch and to brood, though; she didn't *want* to cheer up and stop thinking about it. She wanted to figure it out.

Chloe took out her phone and dialed Brian. If she only did it once, she figured, she could always tell her mom it was someone she needed to get homework from or a study group partner or something.

"It's Brian." His answer was so short and direct, Chloe almost didn't recognize his voice at first. It was very professional sounding—curt, but not self-important.

"Wow, did I just reach Enron or something?"

"Oh, Chloe! No . . ." He laughed, sounding more like himself. "I'm just waiting for callbacks from *every-*one—the zoo, the parks department, animal rescue—even the pound."

"Bad economy," Chloe said, the way she had heard her mother and her mother's friends talk about it.

"Ain't that the truth." He sighed. "So you, uh, want that pattern, right?"

Chloe had completely forgotten about it. "No," she said darkly, "I don't think I'll be needing that anymore."

"Oh." He sounded confused—but was that also *relief* in his voice?

"But I'd still like to see you again."

"Yeah?" he asked cautiously.

"Yeah." She laughed. "You want to go somewhere tonight?"

"Tonight?" There was a pause, like he was looking at his watch or a calendar or something. "Uh, tonight's not *great*. . . . I have to send out a bunch more letters and resumes and applications and stuff. I wanted to get them in the mail tomorrow."

Chloe's ears prickled. There was something odd about the way he was talking, strange pauses—whether it was her new, keen senses or just intuition, she had a feeling he was lying to her. *What's going on with him? He sounds like he's interested, but he keeps sort of putting me off.*

And then it occurred to her.

"You have a girlfriend, don't you?"

"What?"

"Tell me the truth. You have a girlfriend."

"No! *I have no girlfriend*," he said with exasperation. "I haven't had one in *months*. Why?"

"You just sound like . . . I don't know . . . grudging about the whole thing."

He laughed softly. "Chloe . . . I don't mean to be. I'm just kind of anal and obsessive when it comes to setting a goal and a schedule for myself. I'm like a rat, you know? Can't get food until send out one more letter."

"Oh." Chloe looked around in embarrassment, but no one on the bus was listening. "I'm sorry. I've had a weird day. My best friend Amy and I just had this huge fight—" Something finally broke inside her. Chloe swallowed, trying to hold back the tears that were beginning. She turned her face into the window and rubbed her eyes with her knuckle, trying to bruise them away.

"What happened?"

"It's no big deal," she whispered, trying not to sound like she was crying. "It's just like . . ." *I have these new claws, there's this note that says my life is in danger. . . .* "Amy's dating my other best friend and doesn't have time for me anymore, and she doesn't even realize what a bitch she's being." It felt strange to finally say it aloud. She had been thinking it for a while, accompanied with all of the self-doubt that went along with too much introspection. But now it sounded *real*. And even weirder—he had asked her what had happened. He'd asked about what had happened between a girl he'd only gone on one date with and her best friend, whom he had never met. And sounded like he was actually interested. Like he kind of cared.

"I'm sorry. I mean, of course I'll see you tonight."

Chloe smiled through her sniffles. "Can you—are you free now?" She didn't want to tell him how hard her mom had been on her lately—that sounded so high school. Like she was a little girl not in control of her destiny or daily life. *Which is true, but it's fun to dream.*

"Yeah—want to meet at that coffee place by the playground, across from the Peet's?"

"That would be great. I'll see you in a few."

"Okay, be right there."

She got off at the next stop, calling her mom to say that she had to stay after school for extra help with trig.

Twenty minutes later she was hunkered down in a comfy, shabby old chair, sipping a mug of tomato soup while Brian sat across from her, looking concerned. *I could get used to this,* Chloe decided. Even though her own friends were—*had been*—really nice, Brian focused his attention on her in a way she had never really experienced before. The kitty cat hat lay on the table between them, and his hair, rather than being flat, greasy hat hair, was sticking up in tousled dark brown clumps that she longed to run her fingers through and straighten. He had another book this time, a collection of short stories by Eudora Welty.

"It sounds stupid, I know," she said, trying not to sniff. "But Amy's always been the constant in my life. My dad disappears, there's Amy. My mom becomes a complete bitch, there's Amy. Paul acts like a dick to me, there's Amy. Only she's not *there* now, you know? I can't rely on her. She doesn't even answer my messages anymore. And there are . . . other things in my life, too, stuff I want to tell her about. . . . Stuff we definitely would have talked about if things were, you know, normal."

"What kind of stuff?"

Chloe hesitated. She was aching to tell *some*one, and Brian seemed like the sort of person who would sympathize once he believed her. But it was a *big* secret and too soon. Maybe she could tell a *little*. . . .

"Well, like, I fell from Coit Tower," she said, just as abruptly as she had with her mom.

Brian stared at her.

"I mean, she was *there* and everything and took me to the hospital with Paul. . . ."

"What do you mean, you 'fell from Coit Tower'?" Brian demanded.

"I mean, I fell." Chloe indicated with her fingers and the large pepper grinder, making it look like a little person was walking off it and falling.

"From the top? Were you rock climbing?"

"Yes, from the top. No to the rock climbing. Just out the window."

Brian stared at her silently for another moment. Chloe began to feel a little uncomfortable.

"And you're . . . just . . . fine?"

"Pretty much." She shrugged and tried to look nonchalant. "But listen, we were talking about me and *Amy.*"

"And not the fact that you didn't *die*?"

"I think I almost might have," Chloe allowed, thinking back and wondering how much more to reveal. "I was in this place, and it was all dark, and I was sort of . . . *pushed* back into life. Like another fall, off someplace very high."

"Have you told anybody about this?"

"That's what I'm here bitching about!" Chloe snapped. "See, Amy was *there* when I fell, and we never got a chance to talk about it. About what . . . happened, or seemed to happen. It's kind of weird and personal, you know? I really didn't want to talk about it with anyone else. Besides, she believes in the supernatural and stuff, so you know, she would definitely have some ideas about the whole thing."

"I can see why you'd be reluctant to mention it to anyone else. . . . You probably shouldn't, in fact," he said, taking a sip of coffee. It was plain American. Black. No milk, no sugar, no nothing. Chloe found that kind of sexy; it was rough and masculine. She didn't know anyone else who drank it like that except for doctors on prime time. "Your friend doesn't sound very thoughtful." He took a breath and seemed like he was forcing himself back on topic.

"She's never been really . . . *thought*ful." Chloe reflected on it. "She's an introvert and kind of self-centered, but then she'll suddenly come out of the blue and do something great for you when you least expect it." *Like skipping school to go to Coit Tower the day before your birthday.*

"You don't seem to be blaming Paul much for this or saying much about him," Brian observed.

"He's . . . a different kind of 'best friend,' I guess,"

Chloe said. "He's always around, someone you can watch TV for hours with without saying a word, and it's fine. Or sit on the bleachers with and make fun of the jocks. And sometimes he'll open up a little, like he has no problem admitting when he finds things beautiful, like art or nature or stuff. But he doesn't even talk as much as he used to; he's a lot more introverted and difficult. Almost cold. Since the divorce," she realized lamely.

Brian didn't say anything, just raised his eyebrows, like: *Duh.*

"But *I* need Amy, too," she said in a tiny voice.

Brian laughed.

"Of course you do. *She's* the one who can't seem to adjust or make time for you. Have you tried telling her that?"

"Uh, sort of. The squishy emotional thing is hard when there's already distance and you're pissed at someone." She changed the subject, suddenly uncomfortable. "So, anyway, uh, how's the job search going?"

"Oh." He crouched down over his coffee. His brown eyes narrowed and darkened, like he was trying to reheat it with heat vision. For just a moment he didn't look like happy, sensitive Brian. He looked like someone else entirely, someone a lot angrier. "Terrible. And my dad . . . my dad isn't exactly making it easier."

"How?"

"Lectures. Letters. Warnings about my future." He sighed. "He's very Victorian, does the autocrat-at-the-breakfast-table thing. He wants me to do something productive with my life. Like going into the family business."

"What's that?"

"Really. Boring. Stuff. A security company—corporate empire, really—everything from bodyguard supplies to alarm systems—mainly corporate stuff."

"Bodyguards? That sounds interesting!" Chloe leaned forward. She pictured Brian in something *Matrix*-y, black and neoprene-ish, with leather boots. For some reason she couldn't quite *un*imagine the kitty cat hat, but the rest of the image was extremely sexy.

"Most of what he does is contracts. Paperwork, negotiating with big clients, meetings, company analyses, layoffs . . . the usual corporate crap." He smiled wanly. "*Along* with the Kevlar, the Tasers, and the guns. Hence my interest in the whole fish and game department has dropped—did you hear about the cat they have to hunt down in LA? Not my thing at all. Back to guns and other weapons again. No thanks."

"A cat? Guns?" *Wouldn't a water gun work?* She pictured a little tabby up against a firing squad.

"A mountain lion," Brian explained, laughing. It was like he could see exactly what was in her mind. Chloe found herself falling a little bit more in love. "Horrible, really. It attacked a guy jogging by himself at night up in the mountains. He's in really serious condition."

"What was he doing jogging by himself at night in mountain lion territory?" Chloe asked archly.

"It wasn't in a protected park or anything. He was living in a new condo complex they built near the park, and he was just jogging around the neighborhood."

"So lions are supposed to know exactly where their park ends and where public streets begin and avoid crunching on all the big, juicy human hamburgers that stroll through their territory? So they're going to kill it!?" Her voice rose as she spoke.

"Chloe," Brian said, looking around nervously, "it almost killed a person."

"Whose bright idea was it to encroach on mountain lion territory with condos, anyway?" Chloe demanded. "Jesus Christ, what did they *think* was going to happen?"

"All right," he agreed, "it wasn't nice to destroy more of their environment. But the houses and condos are there *now*. They're not moving. How are you going to keep the lions from attacking people?"

"Big fences? Signs that say, Don't Jog at Night by Yourself, Dumbass?"

"You really don't feel anything for the guy who was almost killed?" Brian asked quietly.

"Of course I do." Chloe sighed. "The poor schmuck wasn't really doing anything wrong—aside from buying a new condo recently built up against parkland, which merits *some* kind of punishment. But is hunting down and killing the cat the right answer?"

"The problem is that it's no longer afraid of humans, and now it has a taste of their blood."

"So we have to exterminate anything that's not afraid of us. Yay us, evolved monkeys." Chloe snorted.

"I *said* I didn't want to work for them anymore," Brian mumbled defensively.

He shook his head, clearing the air and changing the topic. "What about *you*? What do you want to be when you grow up?"

Chloe sighed again. "I don't know. I've sort of already ruled out rock goddess and movie star. I really like working at Pateena's, fooling with the clothes and stuff. Seeing what people buy and why."

"So, fashion designer?"

She laughed and shook her head, sending her bob in a neat little flair around her head—which she knew was cute. "No, that's Amy. She's the stylish, crafty one. We always talked about teaming up after school someday— uh, when she finally gives up her dream of being a poet. She would design the fashions and I would manage the store or company: hiring, fixtures, accounts. . . ." Her eyes grew dreamy, then narrowed. "That's why it pisses me off that Lania gets to work the cash register. She sucks, and I totally want to learn that side of it."

Brian's face was blank for a moment. "Oh, is she that girl who keeps making fun of the way I dress?"

"Yeah." Chloe snorted. "Good customer relations, no?"

"No," Brian firmly agreed. "So are you going to get a job in retail out of school?"

"What are you, mad?" Chloe laughed. "I'm going to

college, dillhole. My mom's a lawyer. She'd kill me otherwise. And besides—retail isn't exactly the best way to realize your life's ambition. I don't think Mr. or Mrs. Gap started out dreaming behind a counter at five-fifty an hour. I'll go to college, and if I still want to do this, I'll get my MBA—isn't that what you do?"

Brian shrugged. "My old man always said that MBAs were charm schools for the slow. But he's old-fashioned and kind of an idiot."

Chloe looked at him, realizing something. "Are you the first one in your family to go to college?"

Brian blushed. "I'm not there yet. That's part of the problem. My dad is dead set against it. He thinks it's a waste of money and you don't learn anything *real*. You're a pretty intuitive girl, you know that?"

She smiled, but when she held his eye for a moment, he looked away. *That explains the books—they weren't just to impress me!*

"Feeling any better?" he asked.

"Yeah," Chloe admitted grudgingly. "I still don't know what to do about Amy, but at least I'm not all crazy about it anymore. I think . . . I'm going to have to give her some space to finally figure out for herself how she's acting, even though it's pretty lonely out there right now."

"You're not *completely* alone," he said with a faint smile.

She *had* told him about the tower, hadn't she? Just

like that. And he hadn't freaked out or disbelieved her—he'd just listened. Chloe hadn't told anyone else, not even Alyec. *Someone to talk to . . .* "Any more near-death experiences, emotional crises with my best friend, and fights with my mom, I know who to call."

"I'm your man," Brian said, giving her a thumbs-up and a wink.

For some reason, it gave Chloe pause. The gesture was familiar somehow.

"Uh," she said, a little unsure of what to do. "I guess I should get going before Mom realizes that I've over-stayed after school."

"Yeah." He coughed. "Of course. I'm glad we could meet, though."

Are you? Chloe couldn't be sure.

He stood up and pulled the table out for her to make it easier to get up with her book bag and jacket, another completely Brian thing. He didn't do it with flare or a dramatic gesture, he didn't do it with a hello-I'm-being-chivalrous attitude, he didn't apologize for what might have been construed as a patriarchal gesture by some. He just did it. Courteousness without an agenda. *I could* really *get to like this.* Except for the whole not-seizing-the-moment thing. Was he shy?

Outside, Chloe threw her scarf on dramatically twice—what could she say, she was in full flirt mode and hoping Brian would notice. It was the only knitting project she had ever finished, with odds and ends from her mom's craft bin. In-your-face patchwork and ugly.

"You want to get together again soon?" he asked, shuffling his feet in the cold. "We don't have to do ska. I thought if you wanted, we could go ice skating or something—"

"Kiss me, you idiot," Chloe said, aware of the fall air, the crackling of dead leaves, the *life* in the environment. She reached up for his head.

Brian pushed her back, gently but firmly on the shoulders.

"What?" Chloe demanded, blushing and angry. "Is it because I'm in high school or something? You're only two years older than I am!"

"No—yes." He changed his answer, thinking it was an easy way out. Then he sighed and reverted to the truth. "No, that's not it. I—I just can't, Chloe. Not now."

"Why not?" She stamped her foot, not caring how little girlish it looked.

"I like you a lot—" he started.

"You're gay," she interrupted. "No, wait—*married*. That's why you said you didn't have a *girlfriend*."

"I'm not gay and I'm not married. Chloe, I really do like you. I—" He was about to try and get off with a platitude, but Chloe gave him a warning look. "I *want* you," he whispered. "I just—can't—right now."

"Does this have something to do with your father?" she asked. "'Cause he ain't watching right now, I can tell you that."

Brian's shoulders sagged and a shadow came over his brow. For the first time since she had seen him, he looked like an entirely different person: haunted, conflicted, and most of all *defeated*.

"So what now?" she asked, a little more gently.

Brian sighed. "I don't know."

Chloe wandered home glumly, too down to run. But as she walked past a familiar parking meter and car, it suddenly hit Chloe. The night with the other cat person. He had given her a thumbs-up, too, and turned his head like he was winking.

Thirteen

Chloe didn't have a lot of time to think about her realization immediately; it was pizza night. She and her mom did takeout fairly often, several times a week. But *pizza* was special and they ordered it rarely, keeping the nature of the occasion festive.

Once upon a time a year or so ago, Chloe had gotten all grown up and responsible for a month, trying to make dinner for them at least once a week, but that had been phased out as she and her mom started fighting over things more and more. *I should probably start doing that again. . . .* It was hard for Chloe to remember that her mom was a *person*, often exhausted and with her own troubles, but when she did, she was genuinely sorry.

And sorry she was such a burden.

They got a large pepperoni and split it with no mention of waists, calories, fat, or anything else. Rarely did a slice make it to a plate—one of them would scoop it up and shovel it directly into her face. The television wasn't on.

The whole thing was a little forced, but they were giggling—especially when her mom got a red Ronald McDonald smile on her face ear to ear from tomato sauce.

"Are you . . . okay?" Mrs. King finally asked when the laughter died down.

Chloe shuffled in her seat and played with one of the crusts on her plate, which she always saved for last, like a little pile of bread or pickup sticks.

"Mom, I want to go out," Chloe said quietly. "With . . . guys."

Or at least stop lying about it.

Her mother looked up at her, seemingly impressed with her daughter's new, mature-sounding tone.

"Look, I know you said it was like the last thing Dad asked before he left, but . . . he's *gone*," Chloe said, indicating the two empty seats at the table. "He hasn't been here for the last twelve years. I don't think he has a right to dictate my life from the past."

"I *never* agreed with your father's views about raising you," her mom said, ripping off another slice with more force than she had to. "We didn't agree on *anything* toward the end." She bit and chewed pensively. "Well, we probably didn't agree on anything in the beginning, either, but it was all hidden by the rosy mists of young love. And we both loved *you*."

Chloe didn't say anything, even holding her breath so she wouldn't interrupt her mom's train of thought.

"By the end, you were all that we had in common."

Her mother sighed and smiled sadly at her. "And we began to fight over you."

"So by keeping to the one last thing you disagreed with—you were still keeping Dad here somehow?"

"You watch *way* too much daytime TV," her mother said wryly, but didn't disagree.

"If he loved me so much, it would have been nice if he stuck around a little," Chloe muttered.

They were both quiet for a few minutes, chewing.

Then her mom sat up straighter and looked Chloe dead in the eye, coming to a decision. "You can't be skipping school and falling from towers and leaving hospitals and spending time with boys alone during school hours. Have you *seen* the news recently? About that dead girl, stabbed in the alley? They think her attacker knew her. It's bad enough out there, but you've also been lying to me—how am I supposed to be able to trust you?"

Chloe's first reaction was to argue that that wasn't fair, but unfortunately, her mom had a good point.

"All right," Mrs. King said with resolution. She spoke in her lawyer voice. "From now on, clean slate between us, okay? You can go out and do all the 'normal' things—and don't think I won't be talking with other parents to see what exactly is considered normal. But you can't skip school anymore. You have to tell me where you're going and when. And sometimes, now and then, I will be checking up on you. You don't have a very good track record, young lady." She frowned at Chloe.

"I want to be part of your life, Chloe, and help and pro-tect you—" Chloe tried not to giggle at that part, think-ing about what she had done to the bum. *"Capisce?"*

Chloe nodded. "Agreed."

"Good." Her mother took another huge bite of pizza.

"I got my period," Chloe said brightly.

Her mother choked.

At school the next day Chloe found herself reviewing everything she knew about Brian. The kitty cat hat, how he knew so much about the lions, how concerned he was that she might have talked about her survival of the fall with anyone else, like he was afraid of other people find-ing out her secret. And the thumbs-up just clinched it. *He really* must be *the other cat person!* She couldn't believe she hadn't realized it before. It all made sense, starting with their first meeting and her instant attraction.

But why didn't he just come out and tell her? And why wouldn't he kiss her? Did it have something to do with being cat people? Chloe felt sure he would tell her eventually, that all would be revealed in due time. She couldn't wait. Brian was everything she had hoped for: someone to talk to and someone who could tell her about her cat nature, who could teach her about it.

Making out would be nice, too, though, Chloe couldn't help thinking.

Gradually she thought about the less exciting parts of their conversation. . . . Like really, what *did* she want to be when she grew up? All the answers she'd given him were true, but were they correct? Was going into the fashion industry the right thing to do? Should she look for a higher cause, a nonprofit, something for the good of the world? And what about all those little kid dreams: fireman, astronaut, president. Could she really rule *all* of them out? Was she too young to narrow things down?

I might actually go talk to the guidance counselor, she decided. It was last period of the day; many teachers would already be warming up their cars or having their last cigarette break. And except for National Honor Society members—like Paul—the counselor was definitely an unutilized school resource. He would most definitely be free. Even if she chickened out of actually talking to him, she could go through all of the brochures outside his office. They had seemed kind of lame before, but some of them were put out by companies, she remembered, and spoke about careers within them. Paul had talked vaguely about publishing at one point, when he had given up on the music industry, and had taken a bunch of pamphlets.

She was walking by the newspaper office and found herself instinctively heading toward it—also probably because she was thinking about Paul—before remembering and continuing to walk ahead. She had *no* desire to see either one of the couple of the year.

Too late.

The door opened and Paul was walking out, a dollar in his hand, probably going to the snack machines in the cafeteria.

"Hey, Chloe," he said, a little surprised, but not upset.

"Hey," she said, and stopped walking. But she didn't say anything further, just stood there, looking at him, slightly bored and impatient.

"I heard you and Amy were fighting." He said it with faint surprise, like it was some other people he was talking about, like it was juicy school gossip. He was *almost* preppy today in khakis but with a slim, expensive-looking off-white shirt with red stripes along the seams and a tiny Puma insignia on the back.

"Um, yeah." She tried to sound cool. "Amy was pissed because I didn't want to go over to her place. She blew *me* off when I texted her about lunch and she didn't even read it."

"Oh," Paul said, shifting his weight from one foot to the other. "She didn't tell me about that."

"*Quel surprise,*" Chloe muttered.

"Does it bother you that we're together?"

That was so Paul. Guarded, guarded, silent, then . . . pow! The direct, emotional kicker.

"It's a little weird," Chloe finally admitted. "But that doesn't bother me as much as her—and your—complete disappearance from my life. I mean, she always gets a little caught up in her boyfriends, and you always had the 'secret girlfriend' thing going on. . . . But this is different. We haven't hung out since that weird double-date thing with Alyec. I don't *want* to double date; I want to just hang with you guys like we used to."

Paul nodded, not saying anything.

"A lot has been going on with me recently and she hasn't. . . . Neither one of you has been around to hear it. It's like she doesn't even care anymore."

"I think," Paul said delicately, "she might be a little . . . concerned about your current choice of boyfriends."

Which one? Chloe almost asked.

"*Alyec?* What the fuck, man? I wasn't pissed or rude to her face about Ottavio or that loser Steve who brought fucking *ecstasy* into my mom's house and tried to sell it at my *Halloween* party."

Paul nodded again, getting quieter as she got louder. He did not disagree.

"Alyec is completely hot, doesn't take himself seriously, and doesn't deal drugs. Look, whatever," Chloe said, calming down. She could feel her fingertips beginning to itch again. "*I* think she's acting like a real bitch about everything, and frankly, I don't have time to deal with her shit right now. If she's not going to be around to lend an ear, at least she can keep her distance and shut the fuck up."

Paul raised his eyebrows. The movement didn't touch the rest of his face; he looked a Vulcan or something, with immobile, high cheekbones and eyes so dark you couldn't tell the pupil from the iris.

"I'm sorry about the ranting." Chloe sighed. "I gotta go."

"Chloe—" Paul stopped. "I'm sorry. Don't confuse me with her."

She softened a little. He sounded anxious, genuinely worried.

"I won't." She kissed him on the cheek, amusedly remembering how she'd had the urge to suck face with him a couple of weeks ago. No such desire made itself known now; just warmth and friendliness. *The way it should be.*

Paul smiled.

"Okay, well, see you later?" It was a question, a promise.

He continued on his way to the cafeteria—which was a relief; if he had gone back inside the newspaper office, Chloe would have suspected that he was going to call or text or e-mail Amy. Or worse, that she'd been in there the entire time. As Paul turned the corner, Chloe leaned forward and sniffed. She wasn't sure exactly what she was smelling *for*; if asked, she would never have been able to describe Amy's scent beyond the Anna Sui perfume she sometimes wore. She just assumed there would be some warm, vaguely familiar smell.

But there wasn't. Just Paul, his masculine, slightly acrid smell—not bad, just that he probably hadn't washed the gel out of his hair from yesterday. And his skin—images flashed through her head, but none of them matched or described the smell exactly. Ivory soap, sandalwood; something comforting and deep and good.

Oh, and underneath it all, a package of Cheetos he must have consumed a few minutes ago.

I could be a bloodhound, Chloe thought smugly. Then

she thought about Paul: he only ate crappy snacks when he was nervous. Either it was trig or her and Amy.

She continued on to the guidance counselor's office and began to look at the pamphlets, raising her lip at the army, ROTC, and other military ones. These she took and surreptitiously tipped into the recycling bin. Paul's cousin had been killed in Baghdad—he had joined the army because his father wouldn't send him to an American college and he didn't want to go back to Korea. Just like Brian, except he didn't mind guns.

"Ms. King. You are the *last* person I expected to see here."

Chloe tried not to look up with sneering surprise at Mr. McCaffety. He was *such* a guidance counselor, with visible dandruff and really ugly loafers.

"As opposed to, say, the kids who smoke up in the parking lot at lunch?"

"Good point," he allowed. He took a sip of coffee out of a mug that said World's Best Dad. A blurry shot of his twin daughters was framed beneath the words, an indistinct clue to his humanity, a life beyond these walls. "I meant to say I didn't really expect you to come here of your own volition."

Chloe shrugged, pointing at the rack of booklets. "I don't know what to do." *With my life, my boyfriends, my best friend, the threat on my life . . .*

Mr. McCaffety's eyes lit up.

"Well, I want to get out of here," he said frankly, "but why don't we make an appointment?"

"Okay," Chloe said, a little guardedly. She hoped no

one else heard about this. "I've got second period free Mondays, Wednesdays, and Fridays. . . ."

"Great. How's Friday?"

"Uh, okay, I guess."

"Anything I should research, know about before you come in?"

Research? He's actually going to look up stuff for me? Chloe blushed. "I'm kind of interested in the fashion industry. . . ."

"Ah. Design or corporate?"

"Corporate." This was really weird. He was taking her seriously. What she wanted to do with her life, seriously. Like she wasn't a dreaming little sixteen-year-old with delusions of grandeur.

"Excellent! Well, we'll see what we can find. I'll see you on Friday, then."

"Yeah, right," Chloe agreed in a daze.

"Hey." Alyec caught up to her as she was just about to board the bus back toward Inner Sunset. "Want to come with me across the street? I have to go to the comic store. We can hang out."

Wednesday is comic day. Alyec read comic books? Chloe couldn't help noticing that every new detail about the boy's personality and life revealed him to be—well, more boyish. *If it wasn't for the accent and the looks, he could just as well be an Alex having grown up in the Valley or Idaho or something.*

"I have to work today," she answered, looking at her

watch and trying not to smile. "If it's on the way and we're less than a half hour, I can walk with you."

"Oh, they have them bagged and up at the counter for me," Alyec said easily. He didn't *look* like a comic book reader, like the pale-fleshed males and females who were already hurrying together in a protective band out of the school. Paul was one of them, distinguishable by his slightly healthier skin tone. He waved to her as the group walked by. They were all laughing and arguing and loudly quoting movies and books and television shows. Chloe felt a quick pang of sadness as she watched them go. They were a little clan where everyone was accepted; if one was acting all bitchy—like, say, Amy—there were at least five others with whom one could take solace. *Plus they would probably think my claws were really cool.*

"I would be their goddess," she mused aloud.

"You would be *any*one's goddess," Alyec said without really listening. "Come on. I want to beat the rush." He took her by the hand and led her away. He was wearing a brown turtleneck sweater, precisely fitting jeans, and European-looking leather shoes and looked exactly like a model or a pouty-lipped god listening to the coolest new music on a Virgin ad.

"Do any of the other popular kids know you do this?"

"They accept it." He shrugged. "You and your friends talk about 'popular' a lot," he added, but didn't make a comment or conclusion.

Chloe waited outside the store, less from embarrassment

than claustrophobia; the tiny shop was packed with people. She also felt a little strange: here she was, an actual person with actual weird abilities. She worried that the comic readers could sniff her out or tell that she was different.

"Ach," Alyec said, emerging. "*Superman* looks like it totally sucks this week. Thank goodness for *The Punisher*."

"Well, that's what you get for reading kid stuff," Paul said, coming out the door behind him. To Chloe's surprise, Alyec didn't get upset.

"Yeah, I know." He sighed. "But you know, Superman is a symbol of America, so when I was in Russia, he used to mean everything to me. Rock music. Television. Money."

"Don't you mean truth, justice, and the American way?" Paul asked, a very faint smile on his lips.

"Yeah, whatever. Same thing." Chloe looked back and forth between them, her best friend and her boyfriend, who were really as different as the sun and Pluto, talking easily.

"I guess geekdom is the great leveler," she observed.

"You haven't seen anything yet," Paul answered, grinning. "Just wait until a convention. Well, I gotta go . . ." He faltered. *Pick up Amy,* Chloe realized. "Pick up Amy," he finally said, determined to keep things normal between everyone. Chloe was glad; at least the two of them could still communicate.

"C'mon." Chloe dragged Alyec, who had begun to flip through his brown paper bag of goodies. "I'll buy you some fries." He brightened up and went with her. Like a lot of the popular kids, he never seemed to have a book bag or backpack or anything, not even one of those messenger bags. Chloe wondered where they put all their stuff.

They stopped at the McDonald's a block from Pateena's and she kept her word, although she wouldn't let him eat any that she didn't hold in her lips.

"That's no fair," Alyec said, biting one and kissing her. "You get half."

She stuck a finger in the ketchup and licked it suggestively. "Hey, are you complaining?"

"No." He kissed her again, without a fry to entice him.

Chloe stopped, feeling someone watching her. There was a stopped footstep, a familiar smell. . . .

Brian, she realized.

He stood across the street, staring at the two of them. Hurt was plainly painted across his face.

"Hang on a sec," she told Alyec, who comfortably grabbed the fries and began tossing them down his gullet as fast as he could. She ran across the street.

"What's going on?" Brian asked heatedly, indicating Alyec. Once again, he was all in black, and his eyes were molten and focused.

"What do you mean?"

"With him? What are you doing? *With him?*" He tried keep quiet, but his voice grew louder and louder.

"Brian, you said you couldn't"—she winced at the clinical, grown-up-sounding words—"engage in a physical relationship with me."

173

He looked at her, uncomprehending.

"You won't kiss me!" she finally said, exasperated. "What are you? A friend? Then you shouldn't mind me dating someone. A *boy*friend?" She let the last word drop, not needing to add anything after it.

"I didn't realize it was so important to you—," he began haughtily.

"Don't give me that crap," Chloe retorted angrily. "It's the twenty-first century, I'm a sixteen-year-old girl, and wanting to kiss my boyfriend good night is not weird or horny!"

Brian let his head hang.

"I like you," she said, sighing. "I really do. But I asked you before—what now? What do you want us to be?"

Brian shook his head and walked away, eyes glassy.

Chloe watched him sadly but didn't chase after him. Alyec wandered over to her, seeming to not mind the incident. He was using the last fry to scoop up the last bit of ketchup. "Who's that, another boyfriend?" he asked, unconcerned.

"Uh, sort of," Chloe said, taken aback by his honesty.

"You haven't done anything with him." It was a statement, not a question.

"Yeah? How would *you* know?"

"He's still alive." Alyec grinned at her. "You would tear a boy like that up and spit him back out when you were done."

Chloe smiled weakly back.

Fourteen

Chloe spent the entire afternoon at Pateena's going over and over her and Brian's conversation. She thought she had been extremely mature and handled it surprisingly well, saying all the right things for once. But it had still been ugly and awful, and it had ended poorly.

Marisol noticed her gloom.

"Hey, what's the matter? You usually get this stuff sorted in the first hour," she said, indicating a pile of blouses.

"Remember when I had no one, and you told me to get someone?" Chloe asked, smiling wryly.

"Yeah?"

"Now I have two. One barely touches me and the other—well, he's not exactly Mr. Sensitive Man/Rocket Scientist."

Marisol whistled. "Ah, the tragedies and troubles of high school. *Two* boyfriends. My, my. Well, I tell you what: if you get this stuff done in the next twenty minutes, I'll buy you *un café* to ease your troubled mind."

Chloe couldn't help smiling; her boss was right. From an outside perspective, Chloe was bitching about an excess of good things, too many choices. *Too bad I couldn't combine them. I'd either have a neutered idiot or one hell of a sexy Mr. Right.* That didn't make the way Brian felt any less awful, though. But if he didn't want to see her with another guy, why didn't he say or do something? Was she coming on too strong? Was this new, confident, sexy Chloe too much for him? Did Brian feel he had to make the next move? And more importantly, did Chloe care about him enough to adjust for him? On the one hand, they'd only gone on two dates. On the other hand, she *really* liked him. Maybe it had something to do with him being another cat person. . . .

The coffee Marisol got her sped up her thoughts but didn't make the afternoon go any faster. Neither did "Torn Between Two Lovers," which somehow got played on the speakers at least three times over the course of the afternoon. It was weird how many customers could actually whistle or sing along to it.

Finally the sun began to go down and it was time to close up shop. Chloe called her mom to let her know she would be coming straight home after helping Marisol with the gate. Mrs. King thanked her for letting her know and said that she would be home a little later—they were taking out one of the other lawyers who'd just found out she was pregnant. Chloe didn't feel it was necessary to specifically mention getting fries with Alyec; that had been officially on the way to work from school, more of a detour than a destination.

Chloe steadfastedly refused Marisol's proffered taxi money this time, claiming she was just going down the street to the deli to wait for her mom to pick her up. As soon as Marisol was safely out of her line of sight, however, Chloe leapt up a bench, then a tree, and then onto a roof, determined to make it as close to home as she could without coming down.

One! she counted, making a running leap onto the roof of a nice, long attached condo. It was good for about a hundred feet. *Two!* She leapt off the side onto another house, which was much shorter and farther down than she expected, causing her to roll to break her momentum and keep her legs from breaking. She sprang up at the end, though, making an Olympic-style landing— except for the crouching, catlike, all-fours aspect.

Three! With barely a pause she straight jumped onto the garage of the next house . . .

. . . when she felt a sting on her left leg and felt something rip. She pitched forward, but instinct took over and she cradled her leg as she fell, missing the roof completely and landing on the sidewalk. She looked down and saw ropes of blood stream along her skin to the ground and a cold, sharp metal object with a tip buried in her flesh. She pulled it out, biting her lip at the pain, and held it up to the moonlight.

A throwing star, she realized with disbelief. *Like in ninja movies.* This one had ten points, five large ones, one of which was covered in blood and bits of skin, and five smaller ones in between these, either for decoration or to help it spin. There was something written on it, but before she could get a good look, Chloe heard a faint whir. She dropped her head to the ground against her arms—if she'd had ears like a cat, Chloe would have flattened them. Another shuriken flew by and embedded itself in a tire. *Sssssssht* went the air as it slowly deflated.

Chloe leapt up, flipped, and landed on top of the car.

"Excellent moves," said a voice from the shadows. "I can see someone has finally been training you."

"Who are you? Come out!" Streetlight glittered on glass and metal pebbles in the road. All the houses were dark or the shades pulled so tightly they might as well have been empty. Holes that might have once had trees and bushes in them were filled with beer cans and old toys. This was, as her mother would say, a bad area. A figure hid behind a car so rusted and old, it probably could just have been torn out of the boot that was locked to its right front tire.

A breeze stirred and Chloe sniffed it; this was *not* the cat person from the other night. For some reason she shivered. What was going on?

There was another, near-silent whoosh. Chloe crouched just in time to avoid another throwing star, this one aimed at her neck. She wondered wildly how many he had and turned to run.

Then she realized something: *He's using weapons that he has to* throw—*I'm only in danger as long as I'm* far *from him.* . . . Chloe turned back and ran along the tops of the cars *toward* him. She leapt down to where she thought he was hiding, yowling and screaming to scare him out into the open.

It worked: he threw himself out of her way and into the road.

"Well done."

Streetlight revealed him to be tall and skinny, with tautly outlined muscles on his legs and arms. He wore a dark, almost military-style outfit with a large belt—*for weapons*—and a loose black leather jacket—*for armor.* His hair was so blond it was almost white, pulled back in a ponytail. His eyes were a muddled blue. It was difficult to judge his age, but one thing was for certain: he didn't look entirely sane. His pupils were black pinheads, especially strange considering how dark it was.

He pulled out a dagger and crouched a little, a street fighter. *Like from the game Street Fighter.*

This is crazy, Chloe thought. *No one acts like this.* But it was obvious that the man was serious—and would have to be dealt with seriously.

He was waiting for her to attack. Someone threw a can out a window; it smashed onto the street before rolling into the gutter.

"Can I—help you?" she asked, unsure whether to run away or continue the dialogue.

"What's the matter? No urge to fight? The ancient instinct hasn't awakened in you yet?" the man sneered.

"I had kind of planned on a cocoa and an early bedtime, actually." She circled carefully, keeping a tree between them.

"You almost sound human." With a misdirection of his left hand, he threw the dagger at her with his right. Chloe jumped, but it tore her shoulder as it passed.

He had two daggers now, one in each hand.

"Where do you keep all those things?" Chloe demanded, touching her shoulder. Running now would definitely mean her death: by two quick blades, one in the neck and one in the back.

"I see no one has properly warned you about me," he said, almost disappointed.

"No, no one told me about a crazy blade-wielding psycho—" Then she remembered. *Your life is in danger. Be wary of the company you keep. Be prepared—and ready to run. The Order of the Tenth Blade knows who you are. . . .*

Order of the Tenth Blade? She thought about the shuriken. *Maybe it means that he only has ten blades?* Chloe somehow didn't think that was it. She wouldn't have been surprised if he had a tank hidden somewhere on his body.

"A pity. You should know your executioner."

Chloe shivered again; she felt the hairs on her arms and shoulders rise. Even if he was crazy, he was still serious.

"*My* executioner is probably all the trans-fatties in Oreos and stuff," Chloe countered. *He's going to attack—*

he's going to attack! Any second now . . .

"*Id tibi facio,*" he whispered, and lunged.

Chloe jumped aside, a tenth of a second too late— once again he cut her, but shallowly this time. He didn't move like the homeless guy from the other night; he was fast and well trained—a professional fighter. *Killer,* she corrected herself. He wanted to *kill her.* She leapt again as he brought a dagger down on her and realized she had no time to think, only react.

Her left leg throbbed. It was still bleeding.

He went at her belly with a swipe; she leapt up and grabbed a tree branch, hauling her torso out of the way. He spun, keeping the momentum to hit her as she dropped back down, but she curled in a ball to avoid it. His heel ground against the sidewalk. Whenever she stepped backward, he stepped into her; whenever she leapt to the side, he was there with a dagger.

I have to attack him.

She ducked as he swiped a blade through the air above her head. When she came up, she brought her claws ripping up to his groin. They clanged on something metal.

He laughed.

She had to roll quickly out of the way as he threw a dagger down at her. Chloe saw little blue sparks jump away as it bounced off the pavement with incredible force. She shot out a foot, kicking him neatly in the calf. It made enough impact to give her a little hope.

Fight in, closer, her instincts told her. She was terrified but obeyed. Chloe waited until the last moment and then sprang forward, closing the distance between them, and tried to swipe him across the face with her claws. *Even if you get the slightest bit of flesh or eye,* she remembered her self-defense trainer saying, *the pain will be great enough to distract.*

Only if you hit, though—his arm came up immediately and his wrist blocked her. Chloe brought her knee up to his groin again, planning to shove *up* really hard, figuring that even if he wore some kind of ancient metallic jockstrap or chastity belt or whatever, it would at least hurt a little as it dug into his flesh. At the last minute, though, she leapt up and brought her foot *down* onto his cup and the other foot, too, pushing with all her strength. The way a cat disembowels.

She was rewarded by the first real response from her attacker: he groaned and caught his breath. Then he shot out his fists, one after the other, trying to slash her before she pushed herself away from him. He ripped right down her shirt and through her bra strap, drawing blood underneath in the soft part of her shoulder.

I'm going to lose this fight, Chloe realized, her stomach going cold. He seemed to be able to predict all of her moves—though if it weren't for the exercises the cat person put her through the other night, she wouldn't have survived as long as she had. She would have been lying on the sidewalk, blood running from her throat.

"Give up, blasphemy of nature," he growled. *"Demon!"*

As his slashing blades came closer, she slashed him back, batting at him with her claws and hissing.

He was waiting for that, apparently, and kneed her in the stomach.

Chloe fell over, unable to breathe. *He's trying to goad my instinctive reactions; as soon as I stop thinking and just react, he knows how to get me.* When she fought, he could beat her. He was a good *fighter.* . . .

This gave her the slightest shred of hope. She slowly drew herself up and faced him.

"So I don't scare you?" she asked. *Get a dialogue going.*

"Your kind doesn't scare me," he said with a sneer. "You only disgust me."

Chloe flicked a glance over his shoulder into the street.

"Do *cops* scare you?"

His eyes widened and he turned.

Chloe hadn't thought he would actually do it. Before he realized there weren't any actual police coming, she kicked him as hard as she could in the stomach with the flat of her heel. She spun and did a backward handspring, putting her at least seven feet away from him.

Then she ran, not looking back and putting all of her effort into flight, satisfied with the heavy, thudding sound of his body hitting ground.

Fifteen

She took random paths home, sometimes dou-
bling back and retracing her route for several blocks,
sometimes running in circles. She considered finding
a body of water to run through to hide her scent—
before remembering that *she* was the animal;
her attacker had obviously taken great pride in being
a normal human. *Unless he's a dog,* Chloe mused.
Who was to say that in a world where a girl could
have claws, a guy couldn't have a muzzle and pen-
chant for bones?

The thrill of the fight drove her; part of her
wanted to turn back and finish it. To face death.

But she continued running.

When she finally felt it was safe—after pausing for
a *long* time in public places like convenience stores
and crowded Muni stops, waiting to see if he would
reappear—she went home, carefully locking the doors
behind her. She waited in the kitchen, listening.

After a while the adrenaline in her blood finally died down.

Chloe began to be afraid.

Just because she'd taken a labyrinthine path home didn't mean that he couldn't find her. Obviously he knew who and what she was—how hard would it be to find out where she lived? *How* did he know what she was, for that matter?

He could be coming for me now.

Suddenly she was terrified. It was one thing to be running free on the streets, between houses, out in the open—up to a police station or public place if she had to. But now she was trapped. The windows looked out on a black night spotted with pools of light from other houses and streetlights, which somehow just made the night seem darker, more likely to hide monsters, villains, psychos. Chloe had never really believed in them before, the people who came at you for no reason, from the outside, into your home—that was the stuff of horror movies and urban legends. Now she knew better. It was real.

Chloe turned on all the lights, but the corners still seemed dim and treacherous. She wanted to put on music or the TV, but she was afraid of not hearing him sneak up. She sat on the couch, paralyzed, certain that the next moment was going to bring him smashing into her house with a huge crash.

Just until Mom gets home, she told herself. *She should be here any minute. Just stay calm until she gets home.*

The thought reassured her.

And then she remembered the fight, the crazy, cold look in his eyes, the names he'd called her. What ancient, childlike habit made her believe that her *mommy* could protect her? She didn't even have the speed or claws of her daughter.

A second thought, more gruesome than this one, came: *If he comes here, it's my fault.*

Not only could her mother probably not protect her, but Chloe would have led him directly home, if not now then later—and if her mom got hurt, it would be because of Chloe. . . .

What else can I do?

She reached for the phone. Maybe this guy knew her secret, but he was still a violent weirdo and she had the scrapes and bruises to prove it—she could describe him perfectly to the police and let *them* take care of it. If her attacker raved about Chloe being some sort of "blasphemy" and mentioned her claws—*especially* if he mentioned her claws—they would decide he was a crazy from whom she and the rest of society should be protected.

She dialed 9-1—

What about Xavier?

She paused. Whatever happened to Xavier, anyway? What if he had died? *Not all deaths appear in the obituaries.*

Her DNA was all over his lips and back and shirt. Her fingerprints on his doorknob and phone. If there was an investigation, she would at least be questioned, probably as a prime suspect. What if they examined her? Looked at her claws, checked her fingernails, x-rayed her fingers?

She cursed herself for not following up on him, seeing what had happened. If he hadn't died, the people at the hospital would have questioned him—"Yeah, there was this girl I met at the club; she was the last person I touched before I got sick. . . ." Typhoid Mary. Scratches and boils across his back where she had scraped him. Where her claws would have been, if she had known. She would make an interesting research subject. . . .

She put the phone back down.

I have a secret.

It didn't sound pretty, like a junior high secret crush or journal or juicy piece of gossip. The claws, the expanded senses, the speed, the freedom, the night—she hadn't realized they came with a price. Like the time she'd taken a pull from a bong, when the giggles were over and she'd realized she had *done something illegal*—that if they chose to, any of her friends could have told, and she would have had a police record or gone to juvie hall. She had a secret and it was *punishable*.

Silence overwhelmed the house. Once in a great while a car drove by and Kimmy the shih tzu would bark—Chloe thought about going outside to see if he still acted weird around her, but she couldn't bear the thought of opening the door.

There was a bang and a metallic-sounding scrape as someone threw a glass bottle into a recycling can.

More slowly than she had ever done anything, Chloe moved to the stairway and went upstairs. Every step was forced, every moment balanced. She listened for footsteps outside in the grass or on the pavement beneath the windows. The twelve steps took twenty minutes: she could barely hear over her own heartbeats and breathing.

When she finally got upstairs, she opened her drawer with what seemed like *way* too much noise.

Squeak!

Mus-mus ran from her. She put her hand down and he ran into the corner, cowering. Chloe frowned. She pulled a Cheerio from the sandwich bag and held it out to him. He stayed in his corner. It took almost five minutes for him to work up his courage—and then he only ran forward, grabbed it in his mouth, and ran back into the corner again.

"What's gotten into you?" Chloe demanded. He was her only friend in the house right now; she didn't have the emotional energy for *him* to wig out, too. "Come on!" she said, a little more annoyed, going to pick him up. Then she noticed her claws were still out.

He thinks I'm a cat now. A predator.

She made herself relax, calmed her thoughts, waiting until the claws disappeared.

But when she put her hand in, he still ran away.

Chloe was sitting on the bed, in the same position, staring at the closed drawer, when her mother came in hours later. Chloe didn't move when the car pulled up or the door opened or when she came upstairs.

"Hey." Her mom stuck her head in, face slightly flushed from drink and good times. "You're not in bed yet?"

"I'm going. *Now*," Chloe said with a wan smile. Her tears had dried up a while ago, but they'd left scratchy, salty tracks on her cheeks.

She *knew* it wasn't safer now that her mom was home . . . but somehow still she felt like it was.

Sixteen

Chloe had no desire to go to school or work the next day—lying in bed under the covers definitely seemed like a superior option. *But not the safest.* Public places like school and work were absolutely the safest places to be, and in between she would make sure she was with crowds or other people.

And at home, tonight?

She never wanted to live through an evening of fear like that again. Thinking about it made her want to throw up. She hadn't slept much, jumping up at every noise and lying awake for hours, following each sound to its conclusion: cars driving into the distance, someone—possibly with a *different* malevolent purpose—striding down the midnight street, pausing, taking a piss, and then going on his way. A rat or something small and noisy pushed its food along the ground outside her window, into a hole, for what seemed like half the night.

She surfed the Web for a few minutes before getting ready, looking for alarm systems and door jammers and electronic sentries—most of which seemed to start in the five-hundred-dollar category. Chloe tried to come up with a way of suggesting it to her mom: "Uh, there've been a lot of break-ins recently, and I was wondering . . ." The easiest thing would probably be to get a bunch of those kids' toys that were supposed to guard your locker or room from a sibling and set them up all over the house.

But what about *her*? What if he attacked her again, more sneakily?

Thinking over the fight, she remembered how he had aimed for her throat and important joints—shoulders, knees—and finally the belly. She needed some sort of protection for those places: armor. Chloe took out the music box her dad had given her the last Christmas they were all together; where she kept all of her favorite pieces of jewelry, and the sparkly things she never wore. At the bottom, tangled up in a bracelet she got out of a cereal box, was a chain mail necklace she'd bought at a Renaissance fair Amy had dragged her to years ago. She put it on and looked at herself in the mirror. The steel links made a chain that was only a couple of inches wide, but if she wore it a little loose, then at least it protected the lower half of her neck, the veins and arteries there.

Chloe had no idea what to do about her knees and legs. She played with the idea of wrapping them with Ace bandages, the metal pins all stuck along more vulnerable areas. For her stomach and shoulders the closest thing to protection she had was a leather vest from Pateena's—very seventies and cracked in places. But it was a biker's, thick and strong. She dug it out of her closet and put it on.

Some call me a space cowboy. . . .

Really, all she needed was a ten-gallon hat or a huge belt with a silver dollar buckle. *Actually* . . . She tilted her head. With her bob, a pair of feather earrings wouldn't look too bad, either. Maybe some thick black eye liner, clumpy mascara . . .

"Morning," she called, running downstairs and going right for the door. Her mother was doing a crossword—she never seemed to get headaches or hangovers from nights out.

Chloe realized she was breaking a major, major rule of their new "honesty" pact and felt guilty about it—but what was telling her mom going to accomplish?

"You doing anything after work tonight?" Mrs. King asked, trying to sound casual, not looking up.

Patrolling the perimeter? Setting little traps? Trembling in my shoes?

"Uh, no, not really . . ."

"I thought I would make lamb tonight." She tapped the pen to her lips. "A really nice cut. Will you be home by eight?"

An image flashed before Chloe of her coming in late and finding her mother dead on the floor, broken glass and blood everywhere, the smell of burnt lamb fat from the oven.

"Yeah, absolutely," Chloe answered quickly.

At school, she found she could doze for five minutes at a time—catnap—in class, without anyone noticing. While she felt the urge to snuggle down and sleep for much longer—especially in chemistry, when the sunlight warmed her chair and desk—Chloe found that even the brief five was refreshing. In gym she lucked out: they were watching a film about drunk driving. Chloe managed to sleep for the whole forty-five minutes.

She was woken in Am civ by her phone vibrating. She tried not to sit up quickly, annoyed and surprised out of a deep, dreamless sleep. The number was Brian's.

She wondered if he somehow found out about what happened to her the night before. Or more importantly, if he was going to tell her how much he really liked her and apologize for being so hands-offish and weird. Or maybe he was finally going to admit that he was the other cat person. All these things would be good. *Any* of them. She waited until she was out in the hall after class before calling him.

"You rang?" she asked, phone pressed tight to her ear so she could hear over the crowd.

"Yeah—Chloe, we have to talk." He sounded desperate, serious.

"Sure! Can you meet me before work, at the café near there, on the other side of the street?"

"You can't get out earlier?"

Chloe raised an eyebrow. "I'm in high school, remember? Not the 'real world.' Getting out early means calls to Mom and *consequences*."

"Oh. Right. Okay, then, two-fifteen?"

"I'll be there as soon as I can," Chloe promised. She put the phone back into her pocket.

"Hey, Chloe!" Alyec was waving at her. She smiled and sauntered over, swinging her hips in a half-cowboy-with-spurs, half-sexy walk. "Nice vest. So Keira says you're a complete slut. Is that true?"

Chloe's mouth opened—and then just hung there. She was too stunned to speak. Keira's closest friends were in earshot, listening raptly. Alyec was excellently maintaining a straight face, the still-foreign aspect of his expressions never too revealing.

Then Chloe laughed.

It was such a perfect, stupid high school moment, as far away from murdering psychos, supernatural powers, and mysterious fears as one could get. A complete breath of fresh air.

Alyec smiled, pleased to see her reaction.

"I hear you actually have to have sex to be one," she answered loudly. "You should talk to Scott LeFevre and Jason Buttrick and—well, the whole soccer team. Ask them about Keira."

The girl's two friends sped away like little bluebirds of unhappiness, eager to tell.

"You look so down," Alyec said, running a hand sexily through her hair. She pushed her head up into it, enjoying the feeling. *I hope I don't start purring or anything like that.*

"I . . . didn't sleep well last night."

"You should have called me. I would have come over, and *after* that," he said, grinning devilishly, "you would have slept like a baby."

"You're a complete ass," she said, genuinely meaning it.

"You love it, baby." He leaned forward as if to kiss her but stopped just before, so there was a barely a millimeter between them, and just stood there.

Chloe could smell his skin, clean and warm. It felt like she had just swallowed a double shot of cheap whiskey: burning coursed through her stomach and the rest of her body. She turned her face slightly to move her lips along his cheek—still not touching—almost overwhelmed by heat and desire. But she held back.

Alyec finally pulled himself away. "Whew, strong medicine," he said hoarsely.

"Catch you later, lover boy," Chloe said over her shoulder as she walked away.

This is way *too much fun.*

She saw Amy in the hall a couple of times. They didn't look at each other. Amy made a big deal of looking away. Chloe rolled her eyes. *With friends like this, who needs blade-wielding murderers?*

When the final bell rang, she jogged to the café, making sure she was on the side of the street with the most pedestrians, slowing down to tag along in groups, speeding up to pass on to others.

She breathlessly threw herself into the chair opposite Brian, where he was sitting, brooding, over a cup of something and a biscotti. He was looking even less goth than usual, with creased khakis and shined boots and a black hoodie with the number 10 in red across the front. His kitty cat hat was nowhere to be found.

"Hey," she said.

"Hi."

That was it for a few minutes while she ordered and they waited for her coffee to be brought over. It was tense; Chloe almost tapped her feet in impatience. When they were finally alone, Brian looked at her for a long minute, his brown eyes troubled. He absently fingered the scar on his cheek.

"I think you should stop seeing Alyec."

Chloe blinked.

She thought back to their brief telephone conversation, how serious he'd sounded and troubled . . . and realized that the last time he had seen her was with Alyec. It had nothing to do with him being another cat person. . . .

"Brian, I thought we already talked about this—" Then she stopped, thinking about what he'd just said. These days nothing strange or out of the ordinary—no matter how small—could be dismissed anymore as harmless. "How do you know his name?" she asked quietly.

"What?" Brian asked, flustered, not having expected that response.

"How did you know Alyec's name?" Chloe repeated, standing up. "Have you been following me? *Stalking* me?" she demanded.

He looked around, nervous at her loud accusations.

"Chloe, listen to me," he begged. "You really shouldn't see him. He's not . . . *safe.*"

"I cannot believe you, you . . . *freak!*" she said, slamming her fist down on the table. "You won't commit to anything like a real relationship, and after only a few dates you start accusing other guys of being dangerous? That's *pathetic,*" she spat. "Not *safe?* What would you know about safe? Someone tried to *kill* me last night and you're worried about a goofy foreign sixteen-year-old?"

Brian's face went white. "Someone . . . attacked you?"

"Yeah! I could have been killed. I spent the whole night terrified—he knew stuff about me *too,* Brian. I only have room in my life for *one* crazy stalker."

"Are you okay?" he finally asked.

"Barely!" She took the vest and pulled it and her T-shirt aside. The deep gouge was clean but ugly. "Mofo had daggers and throwing stars and all sorts of weird stuff." She was furious but still owed him thanks. "If it weren't for the moves you taught me the other night, I'd be dead," she said grudgingly.

"That *I* taught you?" he asked, confused.

Oh no . . .

"You didn't . . . the other night . . . ? Come on, this is serious. *Please—*"

But he shook his head, shrugging.

When she realized he really meant it, Chloe was almost overcome with despair. Here she'd thought she finally had an answer to the insanity around her: not only was Brian a great guy, but he would have been someone who could teach her, who could protect her, who could tell her what she was.

And he'd turned out to be none of the above. Just some possessive, crazy freak.

"I have to go now," she said, pushing her chair in.

"No, Chloe . . . don't! Wait—"

But she was already out the door.

Seventeen

She stamped outside and stood there for a moment, unsure of what to do. The longer she stayed there, the more time Brian would have to pay the bill and work up the courage to go after her. Which was the last thing she wanted. For a moment, just a moment, she sobbed, feeling utterly lost.

Then she concentrated on what was she had left: the fact that Brian was a complete jerk. She was so angry, she could spit. She started walking—she had to do *something* with all of the rage inside her. Since it was almost time to go to work, she headed in that direction.

She balled her hands into fists and clenched and unclenched her hands, feeling the claws come in and out. It wasn't exactly soothing, but it made her feel better. Her shoulders felt tight, and Chloe wished she could run like the tiger on those gasoline (or was it oil?) commercials, stretching out with her front legs, leaping, springing off on her back ones. Then she thought about the mountain lions in LA—which made her think about Brian, which made her get all angry again.

"Hey, Chloe," a voice called from in front of her, waking her out of her thoughts. It was Keira, in something that looked like an actual tennis dress, complete with pom-pom socks. But she wore it over a pair of Mavi jeans. Even the other girl's smell made Chloe ill: it stank of seething hormones and irritation and, well, Keira.

She stood in front of Chloe casually, as if just to talk.

"Who exactly were you calling a whore today? In the hall?"

"Go *away*," Chloe said, trying to step around her. *Like I need this on top of everything else.* She felt like the fuse in her was half a centimeter from the pipe bomb.

"No, I'm really interested." Keira tossed her hair to the side, exhibiting all of its shades, roots, and layers. "Were you implying that *I* slept with Jason and Scott—and the whole soccer team?"

The bomb ignited.

Chloe turned, eyes flashing. She opened her mouth. A sound came out of it, deep and guttural and raw, from the bottom of her throat. Not exactly human. A warning.

Keira's face went white and she took a step backward.

Chloe walked around her, continuing to Pateena's. She was close to clawing the next person who tried to talk to her.

I'm going to pay for that later, though. As soon as she recovered, Keira would get on the phone to everyone and tell them what a freak Chloe King was, besides being a gossiping, lying rumormonger. But Chloe was pretty sure she wouldn't use the actual word *rumormonger*. It was several syllables too long for the field hockey star's vocabulary.

Chloe managed to calm down enough by the time she got to the store to punch in civilly and grab one of the doughnuts Marisol had thoughtfully brought in for them, even remembering to thank her. They were Halloween-themed ones from Dunkin' Donuts, covered in little black and orange candy bats and pumpkins. Chloe had forgotten about the holiday coming up; it was Amy's favorite.

She felt the urge to growl again.

Trapped within the store, the smell of recently dry-cleaned and bleached cotton and polyester enclosing her, Chloe found her thoughts similarly trapped. She *still* knew nothing about her attacker or the other cat person. She had no new way of protecting herself and her mom. She had no intention of telling her mother about the attack, either, which meant she was already violating the agreement between them. She had no one to talk to. Not anymore.

Chloe found herself attaching labels with the punch gun harder than she had to, putting holes in more than a few pairs of pants.

And this is where I met Brian.

"Awww. Is the little high-school girl all PMS about something?" Lania asked, pouting out her lip and looking down at her. "Whatsa matter, didn't get elected prom queen?"

Chloe considered how Lania's looks would improve with the addition of a plastic tag permanently fixed to her lower lip.

"Leave me alone," she muttered. It was almost a plea; why was it that when everything was at its suckiest, people like Lania and Keira suddenly decided it was their day for free torture? She didn't want to lose her temper again. Several people were in the store, and a leonine roar would certainly be noticed.

Lania shrugged, kicking Chloe's pile of jeans out of the way as she left.

Chloe took a deep breath, picked up another pair, and aimed the gun at it—but she was gripping too tightly and it misfired, jamming. Without thinking, Chloe raised it above her head to dash it against the floor—but stopped herself just in time.

She had to get out of here. Her mood was not improving.

Chloe carefully restacked the jeans, reset the gun, and found Marisol in the back.

"Uh." She coughed. Would she stick to her new honesty policy? "Marisol, I don't think I can keep working here today."

The older woman looked up at her, eyes narrowed, maybe searching for physical signs of illness, the only fathomable reason an employee would say such a thing.

"Are you okay?" she finally asked.

"Not . . . really," Chloe didn't give any further explanation. *Ask me no questions. . . .*

"Okay," Marisol said grudgingly. Her eyes flicked to a couple of black-and-white monitors that were linked to security cameras in the store. Chloe realized she was trying to tell her that she had seen the way she had been behaving. "I like you, Chloe. But I don't have time for crazy teenagers. This is a business I have to run, not day care."

"I understand," Chloe mumbled. *If only she knew what was going on. . . .*

"I think we'll be okay; it hasn't been that busy. Take the rest of the week. But I expect to see you back on Wednesday—if not, don't bother ever coming back."

"Thank you," Chloe said with all her heart.

"All right. See you next Wednesday." The woman turned her back; their discussion was over. Chloe grabbed her jacket and ran outside, rejoicing in the clean, fresh feeling of the sun on her.

But she still wanted to pound something. Where could she go? What could she do to shake this foul mood, this incredible rage?

Alyec.

He might not be the best conversationalist, but he would definitely take her mind off things. But where would he be? She had never seen him with a cell phone, wouldn't know his number if he did have one. She checked her watch—it was only three-twenty; there was a good chance he was still hanging out with his usual crowd of friends somewhere in or near the school.

Chloe ran all the way back and paused outside the main exit. Sniffing. Before she knew what she was doing, she had her nose in the air, trying to catch his scent. . . . *There!* Was that it? She waited as the breeze shifted direction, closing her eyes. A thousand different . . . not images exactly, but feelings and suppositions filtered through: Was that a cat? Was someone angry? Someone hadn't bathed in a while. . . . Something alien, animal, small . . . Squirrel? Rat? She couldn't name the scents; there was no vocabulary for them. But they were recognizable and learnable, like faces and sounds. She could have stayed there for much longer, letting these things fill her—like a dog, she realized, sticking its head out the window, or even that dumb little shih tzu, who always smelled up and down her arm before letting her pet him, as if to see where she had been and who she had seen that day.

There again! That *was* him! Like the smell of his skin this morning, masculine and unmistakably *Alyec*. She followed it, finding it hard not to also follow her instinct and move her head around against the building and even along the ground to follow the trail. But, there were still students around, and her reputation for weirdness had already been established enough that day.

Chloe paused at an intersection, checked the scent, and was rewarded for her guess: it led to the smaller basketball gym. She slowed down at the last minute, hearing other voices, smelling mixed signals, male and female.

She strolled in, like she had just been walking by, knocking on the door as she went.

Alyec sat like a benevolent king among his admirers and friends. Everyone was gathered around and below him, on lower risers, talking and laughing and tossing a basketball. Alyec was trying to learn how to spin it on one finger like the other Americans, causing a lot of giggles. Keira wasn't there. *Thank God.*

He saw her come in. There was no hesitation: he rose with the ease of a reasonably graceful human, tossed the ball to some cute little girl thing, and jumped down, slapping hands and giving high fives as he went.

"Gotta go, catch you all later."

Someone began singing, "Alyec and Chloe, sitting in a tree. . . ." It wasn't even mean, but it annoyed Chloe nonetheless. Who were these *little people* who just commented and talked about her life like that?

"Hey, beautiful." He didn't kiss her perfunctorily like other boyfriends might have—like Brian should have. Like all of their interactions, it was as if such a gesture was too banal for the two of them. He just raised his eyebrows, waiting.

"I want to do something *bad*," she said, half joking.

He looked at her, trying to evaluate her mood. Then he took her hand. For a moment Chloe was afraid he'd taken what she'd said the wrong way; the last thing in the world she wanted was friendly physical contact. Right now the idea left her nauseated.

Alyec began striding down the hallway, pulling her behind him. "We'll blow your steam off," he said as she hurried to keep up with him. "I promise."

He took her to the tiny parking lot in the back of the school, to the even tinier seniors' parking section. The nearing-sunset light was extraordinary, both softening and carefully outlining every shape and color; its heat caused the smell of decaying leaves, tar, and dusty metal to slowly seep into the air. He led her to a tiny hatchback the color of dull copper, old and rusting.

"This is *yours*?" Chloe asked, surprised. "You're not a senior—"

"Is a *great* car," he said, lapsing into broken English in his excitement. "Rebuilt with eight-cylinder engine. Standard shift. Very pure."

"It's yours?" she asked again, noticing he hadn't answered.

"I have always loved the old hatchbacks," he said, taking out a key and opening the driver's side door. "There are a few problems, of course. Like, a few keys will open almost all models." He stuck his leg out of the car for balance and leaned in, fiddling with something underneath the steering wheel. "But you can get in and tinker and really know what you're doing, you know? No computers or that kind of crap."

There were a few short and unpromising-sounding clicks and growls, then something caught and the engine started. He leaned over and unlocked the passenger door.

Chloe opened it, having to pull harder than she thought; it might be a tiny car, but it felt like it was made completely out of lead, and the door didn't swing too easily. She fell down into the low seat, which still retained most of its original—leather? Vinyl? —cover, patched here and there with duct tape.

She looked at Alyec.

"This isn't your car, is it?"

He smiled at her and backed them out of the parking lot.

Chloe didn't know the first thing about cars and very little about actual driving—her mom had let her practice in the Passat once in a while, and she was signing up for driver's ed that spring. But even so, two things were apparent even to her: the little car was accelerating much harder and faster than it should have been able to, and Alyec had obviously not learned to drive in America.

They bounced forcibly up and down in the car; other than springs in the actual seats themselves, there didn't seem to be any form of suspension. She opened the window and grabbed the sill for support and found herself laughing. *Bonnie and Clyde!* Stolen car, infinite anger, open road. This was *exactly* what she needed.

She didn't bother asking where they were going; he seemed to have an agenda. They swung around corners so hard Chloe could have sworn that the two outside wheels lifted up, and while they didn't actually *run* any red lights, she saw them turn as they passed underneath.

Whenever that happened, Alyec kissed his fingers and touched the roof.

"Sometimes," he hollered—his window was down, too, and the engine was incredibly loud—"San Francisco really sucks. You have to get out! It's too . . . claustrophobic."

With a buzz they turned down the 101 and were zooming over the Golden Gate. It was a beautiful end-of-day panorama: the sky was darkening to a clear, pollution-free blue, and elongated puffy clouds rolled by, lit orange from underneath. The colors of the fading green hills in the distance deepened, and the water below looked violent and dark. The bridge itself glowed an almost rusty, bloody red.

"Ha!" Chloe laughed aloud, loving it. Alyec grinned at her and stepped on the accelerator.

They flew down the other side of the bridge and took the first exit, heading toward Sausalito. She and Amy used to go there all the time to shop and hang out along the water—but both had found it dull recently (as Paul always complained it was). Old people and weird tourists and boring shops. But Alyec wound down a road she hadn't been on and up a street that could only be described as *extremely* well paved, like out of a poster: tar hidden by a gravel-topped surface, the lanes curving gently down from the center of the road, where two lemony perfect stripes shone.

"Where are we?" Chloe shouted.

"Where all the rich assholes live," Alyec yelled back.

"I thought that was San Jose."

Alyec thought about this. "*Old money* rich assholes!"

He made a left and pointed. Chloe's jaw dropped at the sight of the house in front of them.

It was like an estate out of some English film, a giant stone-and-wood manor, rising several stories in the middle. Lower wings flanked either side. The roof was slate. The great lawn that sloped down the road had to be several acres at least and was protected by a tall and spiky old-fashioned fence, gate, and guardhouse. A gravel driveway gently rolled up from there to the front door, ending in a circular roundabout whose center was a fountain. Every piece of greenery was immaculately trimmed, and dotting the lawn were topiary and even the occasional fountain.

"Oh my God . . . It's *beautiful*," Chloe breathed. "I had no idea there was anything like this around here."

"It is not mentioned ever in *House and Country*, if that's what you mean," Alyec said wryly.

Christ. "Who owns this place? Bill Gates?"

Alyec shook his head. "Sergei Shaddar. He's the guy who bought the old market downtown and turned it into a multiplex. A true capitalist pig-dog. And a distant relative on the American side of my family." His face went dark for a moment. "He is the one who wouldn't put up the money to bring me and my family over."

"What a douche bag! I can't believe he spent it all on this instead."

211

"Yes, well, who knows," Alyec said airily. "Someday, maybe it will all be mine. He isn't 'married with children,' as they say."

He turned the car around and drove slowly back down the road, letting Chloe get one last good look at the beautiful house. She sighed. It was a complete world away from her and her troubles, a little fantasy kingdom of rich people and beautiful things and rich-people problems.

Noticing her silence, Alyec reached over and handed her a solid pewter flask with Russian words on it. She had no idea how he could have kept it on his person with the jeans he was currently wearing, extra tight around the ass. But she pulled from it generously. It wasn't vodka, as she'd expected, but something dry, deep, and stinging.

"Do you know how hard it is to get bourbon in Russia?" he asked when she coughed. Chloe gave him a smile, but it was weak. "Oh, you're getting all depressed."

"I wish—" She stopped, thinking about her birthday cake. "I don't know what I wish. I wish life was simpler," she finally said. "I wish we could hang out longer."

Alyec chewed his lip for a moment. "We need one last thing to cheer you up before you go home." Then he brightened.

"Chloe King, have you ever 'caught air'?"

Eighteen

In a dark room with no name, a circle of robed figures gathered.

Nine sat around an ancient wooden table lit by flickering lanterns that marked its circumference. Behind and above them, torchlight cast monstrous shadows onto the ornately tiled stone floor below.

A black-and-white monitor sat on the table, adding its sickly light to that of the flames; the main character in its silent movies was a girl engaged in all sorts of normal girl behaviors—as well as some that were not so normal.

One of the robed figures at the table spoke. "You see: already she has become dangerous—and it has been only days since she perceived her true nature."

"I hardly believe that defending herself from the onslaught of a street ruffian constitutes a dangerous personality," said another voice, old and female.

"But see who she keeps for her company," a third,

ancient male voice cackled. A skeletal hand reached for-ward. His fingers might as well have been just bone for all the good his dry, shrunken skin did; it clung to every detail, bump, and crevice. As if to magnify the deteriora-tion, a bold ring with a giant black stone sat above the knuckle of the index finger. All looked to where he tapped on the glass of the monitor.

A young man was kissing the girl, on a bench outside a fast-food restaurant.

"Is the Russian still next in line?"

"We have no reason to believe otherwise."

"This is all moving too fast," the first speaker said, shifting in his seat. "Novitiate, you had said merely that the two knew each other. And that should anything arise, you would immediately . . . intercede."

"I did my best, Primary," a young voice from the benches said dully.

"Yet you failed. You also failed to positively determine whether she is the One the Rogue believes her to be."

"First you want me to befriend her, then you want me to see if she dies when I stick a knife in her belly. I didn't think that was part of my mission."

"Did she *tell* you anything? Anything strange at all—about her past, about some experience as a child, some miraculous survival or near-death experience?"

There was a long pause.

"No, sir," the novitiate said finally.

"I'm afraid you're far too close to the situation to be

able to react rationally. You are off the case; we will let the Rogue handle things his own way."

"But sir—let me try one more time. She's a good person—raised by *humans*. The Rogue will just *kill* her! He's mad—"

"Alexander Smith is a valiant member of the Order. He does his duties well and with zeal—let us not forget this. Above and beyond our own orders, he feels his way is directly ordained by God. Let him be, and God will determine the outcome."

"This is just murder, not the way of God," the young man spat.

"Novitiate, the Order of the Tenth Blade has *not* carried out its mission of protecting people from the feline scourge for a thousand years just to throw it away for the misguided urges of one infatuated adolescent! Am I clear?"

Another long pause.

"Yes, sir."

There was a moment of silence as everyone reflected on this.

"So our action is decided," said one.

"So it is recorded," said another.

"As we have done from ages past, as we shall ever do," chanted all of the figures.

Slowly they rose and filed silently out of the dark room. All except one—the young one who'd spoken, whose knees shook and who scratched at a scar on his cheek.

"It's all for the best, son," the oldest man said, hanging back and patting his shoulder with a skeletal hand. "I know it's hard . . . but there's no future there. Look at that poor Greek boy—you don't want to end up like Mr. Xavier Akouri, do you?"

Nineteen

In fact, Chloe had never "caught air" before, even though she had lived almost her whole life in San Francisco. Amy had tried once or twice, using the car Paul's brother let him borrow occasionally, a really tacky job with purple lights all over the place and a few too many spoilers. But as much as Amy pretended to be a badass, she'd never really gotten up the courage—or the speed.

Alyec had no such issues: he jammed the accelerator at the top of a good hill. But when they raced over it, the car just sort of bounced up and down. Alyec swore and tried again, swerving around corners and running a red light to build up speed. Winds tore through the windows. The city had just entered darkness and the lights were all on, but the afterglow of the orange sunset remained. It was a wild-feeling night.

I can't believe we're doing this. Chloe was so excited, she actually clapped as they approached the intersection.

"And . . . now!"

Suddenly she felt weightless. It only lasted a moment; her body strained against the seat belt and they crashed down *hard* onto the street again, causing her neck to whip forward and back.

She wasn't sure if all four wheels made it into the air, but it certainly felt like it.

It all happens a lot faster than on TV. She sighed, wishing they had gone slow mo through the movement, like they were on camera.

Alyec zoomed back to Inner Sunset. As they drove past the school parking lot, someone—with the build of a senior jock—was screaming, "Where's my *car*? Where's my goddamn *car*?" Alyec and Chloe sank down in their seats, giggling, but the owner's back was turned as they passed him.

"Where do you live? I'll drop you off before returning this."

"You don't know where I live," she said slowly, savoring the way it sounded, how it felt. He didn't know her other boyfriend's name, he didn't know what she really was, and he didn't know where she lived. Just a slightly more psychotic than usual average teenage boy. Simple. It was a nice thing.

"No, how could I?"

"Forget it," Chloe said, smiling, pointing where he should turn.

He slowed down as she tapped the windshield, indicating which house was hers.

"Hey," Chloe said, turning to look at him. *"Thanks."*

"No problem. You see? I'm not just a sexy boy. I also like doing dangerous and stupid things."

"Yeah?" She smiled.

"Yeah," he answered, leaning over. He very gently bit the bottom of her right earlobe, tugging it, deftly avoiding her piercings. Then he kissed her neck. Chloe shuddered. *"Next* time," he whispered.

Chloe's eyes widened, but she didn't say no.

Inside, her mom was wrestling with butcher's twine tied awkwardly around an incredibly primitive-looking hunk of lamb. She was tying a knot, holding one end in her teeth. Chloe went over to put her finger on the knot to make it easier for her, but Mrs. King shook her head emphatically.

"'Ot ohtil oo 'ash 'or 'ands."

Chloe sighed and ran them under the faucet before returning to help. At one time—during her brief stint as a vegetarian—the sight of meat like that, especially weird meat, especially weird meat from a baby animal, would have completely grossed her out. She couldn't help noticing her stomach growl, however, and had to actively resist the urge to pick off bits of the tastiest-looking raw fat and pop them in her mouth.

"There." Her mom put her hands on her hips and admired her work. She indicated the oven with her chin and Chloe opened it, feeling *very* nice heat waft out.

"Should just be forty-five minutes or so. I bought some couscous to go with it. Hey, are you feeling all right?"

Chloe looked up, surprised by the sudden change in conversation topic. Come to think of it, now that the wild car ride was over, she felt a little let down.

"Did something happen at work?"

Chloe took a deep breath. "I didn't go to work. I . . . hung out with my friend, Alyec. He gave me a ride home."

Mrs. King raised her eyebrows.

"Marisol gave me the rest of the week off," Chloe explained quickly. "I didn't feel like—I couldn't do it."

"Don't flake out on this," Mrs. King warned. "This is only your first job. If you get bored with this, and the next, and . . ."

Chloe just looked at her, patiently waiting for her to finish. It was probably the complete lack of *any* response from her daughter—much less an angry one—combined with Chloe's exhausted look that made Mrs. King trail off, giving up the lecture.

"Are you getting sick?"

No . . . But she realized she wanted to leave her options open. So she shook her head without saying anything, a weak protest at best.

They had a quiet night of lamb and couscous and a salad with feta cheese, working the Greek theme. Her mom let her have a glass of wine, something fruity, white, and Middle Eastern. It put Chloe right to sleep when she curled up on the couch next to her mom, who was flipping back and forth between CNN and Animal Planet.

Chloe knew she should have been more alert, but she was exhausted, her belly was full, and she felt cozy and warm.

"Well, what do you know," were the last few words she heard before dozing off. "Baby elephants suck their trunks just like human babies suck their thumbs. . . ."

When she woke up the next morning, Chloe was still on the couch but stretched out, with her own pillow under her head and her own comforter covering her. Her mom was already up and getting ready for work.

"How do you feel today?" she asked, leaning over Chloe and putting the back of her hand to her daughter's forehead. "When I tucked you in last night, you were burning up."

Chloe felt fine.

Holy shit, did I help Alyec steal a car and catch air with it yesterday?

How many more times, she wondered, would she be struck the next day by the weird things she had done the night before? And frankly, thinking about the car theft, she felt sheepish. What had gotten into her yesterday? Was she really that mad at Brian? He was just an idiot, after all. . . . Why did she do these weird things when she was around Alyec?

"Uh . . ." Chloe started to sit up, then fell back on one elbow, as if she were woozy.

221

Mrs. King sighed. "I'll call the school. I shouldn't have let you drink anything last night. Or I should have at least made it red. That's supposed to be good for headaches and colds." She fluffed Chloe's hair. "I'll call you later. Call me if you need anything—do you think you'll be okay at home by yourself?"

Ah, here it comes. Chloe saw the worry and the single-mom guilt shadow her mother's stony eyes. Should she stay home with her sick daughter? That was what *her* mother would have done. *Well, her mother didn't have a job, but whatever.* At least Chloe's mom was always very careful to keep her adult doubts and worries and psychoses to herself and never burden her daughter with them.

Of course, she couldn't help projecting sometimes.

And she would worry a hell of a lot more if she knew about the attempt on her daughter's life.

"Don't worry," Chloe reassured her, wondering vaguely how the whole mother-daughter thing had flipped around so quickly in the last few weeks and wondering when they would flip around away from each other again. "I'll call Amy." *Yeah, right.* "She can come over right after school with stuff if I need it. I'm probably just gonna sleep here for the next few hours anyway."

"Okay," her mom said, sounding unsure. She leaned over and kissed Chloe on the forehead. "Feel better."

And with the clank of a Coach purse, Italian attaché, and Kenneth Cole heels, she was gone.

Chloe waited on the couch for a while before deciding

what to do. There had been enough time since the attack for a little distance; she wasn't as terrified to be alone at home as she had been the first night. This day would be a good test: if her assassin meant to track her down and attack her at home, there would be no better time. She was by herself and the neighborhood was quiet.

But even if she *did* stay at home all day, it certainly wasn't going to be in a prone, vulnerable position lying on the couch. She could follow up on Xavier more, maybe call him. And what exactly *about* Xavier and Alyec? Were these urges—all the way from sexual to self-destructive to simply destructive—*normal*, or did they come with the claws, the speed, and the sudden desire to eat raw meat?

She flexed her hand and watched her claws *sslt* out. She held them up in a ray of sun that beat its way around the curtains and plants. On the one hand, the claws looked "normal": shiny, off-white, with little bits of calluses and dead skin around them at the base. On the other hand—paw—they looked as freakish and alien as the first time she'd seen them.

"What else do you bring?" she asked them aloud. Still no tail, thank God. That would have been harder to hide, and she couldn't imagine it suddenly disappearing somewhere up inside her body. She looked at her feet—her mom had removed her socks sometime during the night. Chloe hadn't even felt it—was that because she'd been dead asleep or because her mother's scent and touch and little sounds were familiar, nondangerous? Had she somehow known instinctually, even in her sleep, that she was safe? Amy's cat would often spend the entire day sprawled at the bottom of the bed. You could pet him as hard as you wanted and he would stretch, never quite open his eye, and continue sleeping.

Or did I just completely pass out? A much scarier thought.

She spread her toes pinkly in the sunlight. Then she flexed them. No claws emerged. Was this it, then? No more physical changes?

She got up and stretched, enjoying the feeling of morning warmth.

Then she went upstairs to brush her teeth and stuff. But before she did, she remembered one task she had to take care of: *Mus-mus.*

She went into her room and opened the drawer. Mus-mus came running forward, eager for a treat. Chloe dropped in a Cheerio. It bounced. The delivery and noise startled Mus-mus for a second, who was used to much gentler treatment. Chloe put her hand out slowly, extending a finger toward the little mouth. He leaned forward, sniffing. Then he squeaked, dropping the Cheerio, and ran away.

"You don't like cats, even nice ones . . . ," Chloe whispered. Just one more thing that came with her changes, along with the violence. She bit her lip, feeling a tear well up in the corner of each eye.

"Okay, Mus-mus." She reached forward to pick him

up; he was so desperate to escape her grasp that she had to extend her claws and very delicately close them around him like a cage. She held the mouse up to eye level, regarding the terrified little thing that had been her closest confidant as of just a few days ago. "Goodbye," she whispered. "And good luck."

Then she leaned down and opened her hand near the base of the bed. Mus-mus didn't hesitate at all, shooting forward and under the bed as soon as he could. Chloe sighed again, knuckling the tears out of her eyes. She carefully placed a little pyramid of Cheerios on the floor in case he needed a good start.

I'm gonna miss you.

She took a shower, trying to wash away everything she felt and start the day again. She put on her tank top and a pair of jeans, not bothering with undies. *Cats don't wear underwear,* she told herself but didn't even manage a smile. She adjusted her bra. *This cat has to wear something supportive on top, however.* She couldn't imagine having six or eight teats the size of her own.

Chloe wandered around, straightening some things, cleaning out the fridge for her mom, channel surfing. Overwhelmed by depression, she lay down on the couch.

Would I give up the claws if it meant no more crazy attacks on me, and life would return to normal, and Mus-mus would come back? Even if she had the choice, she wasn't sure what the answer would be.

•   •   •

A hesitant knock at the door jolted Chloe out of a long, dreamless sleep. She looked out the window, fingering the chain mail necklace at her neck.

It was Amy and Paul.

Chloe frowned, not sure she was ready for this. But she went downstairs anyway and opened the door.

"Chloe," Amy said. Her and Paul's eyes immediately took in the sexy tank she was wearing—and then focused on something particular near her left shoulder, causing them to gasp.

"Uh, your mom called us. Amy, I mean," Paul explained as Amy stared, still fixated on the wound from the other night. Chloe had cleaned it out in the shower and put antibiotic on it, but it was still huge, deep, and red. Healing fine, just ugly. "She said you were sick."

"Yeah, uh, come on in." Chloe opened the door all the way, turning to go into the room first. Her two friends followed meekly. "Want anything? Coke? Diet Coke?"

"Coke," Paul said absently.

The stillness in the room was museumlike; it was twilight and everything was dusky, dusty, dim. Like a grandmother's house. Noises dropped and disappeared into the room like drops into a flat black lake, absorbed instantly.

"What happened to your arm?" Amy finally asked.

Chloe turned from the fridge and tossed Paul his Coke.

"I was attacked on the sidewalk the other night," she answered flatly.

"By the bum," Amy supplied hopefully.

"No, someone else. Someone with a knife. Someone who seems to be *stalking* me."

All three were silent for a moment. Amy seemed to disappear into the gigantic puffy silver coat she wore—somewhere between pimp and London DJ chic. Her hair was up in knots and she had a thin lime green scarf thrown about her neck. Paul looked far more casual—though just as ill at ease—in jeans and a leather jacket, surprisingly normal for him.

"Is it someone you know?" Amy finally asked.

"No."

"Have you called the police?"

"Not yet."

Amy must have sensed something in Chloe's tone; she didn't follow up with the obvious, "Why not?"

"I guess we have a lot of catching up to do," Amy said slowly.

"Yeah?" Chloe asked, sounding like she didn't care.

"I didn't realize—you didn't tell me. . . ." There was a long pause. "I really haven't been there for you, have I?" Amy said softly.

"Not really," Chloe agreed, but there wasn't any malice in the way she said it.

"Paul told me how you felt." Amy suddenly laughed, forced. Paul looked down, embarrassed. "*Paul* told *me*. How *you* felt. That's a first." She was right: usually one of the two girls was demanding that the other talk to the impenetrable Paul. "I flaked, I know—and then I got pissed because you

227

were dating Alyec. *And* this other guy. It was like you suddenly had this whole life apart from me."

"He*llo*?" Chloe indicated Paul.

"I know, I know." Amy sighed.

"I can leave . . . if you guys want," the boyfriend in question suggested, a little annoyed that he was being referred to as a distraction.

"I thought you would be overjoyed we were together, like celebrate it or something," Amy continued. "It's like—you know, perfect. Your two best friends, dating."

"I'm going to . . . uh . . . go to the bathroom," Paul said, getting up and leaving.

"That's pretty egomaniacal of you," Chloe said, sort of regretting that she hadn't minced words, sort of glad she'd said it the way she had. "I've never really dated *anyone* and you've had a string of boyfriends—and now you and my only other close friend have decided to see each other exclusively? How do you *think* I felt?"

"Is that why you suddenly started dating all these guys?" Amy said, heat rising in her voice.

"There aren't 'all these guys.' There's Alyec, who's fun and a great kisser, and Brian, who I met at the shop. Oh, and Xavier, this guy I met at the club the night after I fell when I was totally alone and felt weird and I tried calling you everywhere and you were busy with Paul."

Amy's mouth opened as if to say something, but nothing came out.

"I don't really count him," Chloe admitted. "I've only

seen him once since that night." *And he was at death's door.*

"Why didn't you tell me at dinner when—" Amy suddenly broke off, remembering the birthday pizza and how eager she'd been to talk about *her* experience with Paul the night before.

"You looked like you needed someone to listen to you," Chloe said quietly. "I didn't think what I did with Xavier was as important as what was going on with you two."

Amy's eyes grew wet and glassy.

"I'm *sorry*," she finally said, trying not to cry. "I know I haven't been there for you *at all*, and I felt guilty about it, but I was angry and busy with Paul, and the longer we went, the guiltier and angrier I got. . . ."

"It's okay," Chloe said, trying not to smile. Typical Amy. Overemotional but genuine to a fault—if you pressed her long enough. Amy grabbed her in a big bear hug that made Chloe grunt in surprise, the breath knocked out of her.

"Wait, isn't two attacks on you in one month kind of weird?" Amy suddenly asked, wiping her tears off.

"You don't know the half of it," Chloe said with a wry smile.

"Hey." Paul appeared in the doorway. "Why don't we walk across the bridge, like we used to?"

Amy and Chloe looked at each other. *Why not?* Chloe thought, trying not to focus on how "used to" was less than a month ago.

•　　　•　　　•

On the bus ride to Golden Gate, Chloe filled them in on the details of Alyec—minus the car theft—and Brian, focusing more on the latter and how she was really disappointed he'd turned out to be such a loser. Both her friends were disturbed when she told them about how he knew Alyec's name and told her to stay away from him.

"Isn't that a little weird, two stalkers so close together?" Paul asked, unknowingly echoing Amy's previous question. "You don't suppose . . ."

"That Brian hired a knife-wielding maniac to frighten me?"

"Or Alyec," added Amy quickly. She had granted that the popular boy might not be the root of all evil in the universe, but she hadn't given up hoping that he might be.

Chloe and Paul ignored her.

"Maybe you *should* call the police," Paul suggested in his "serious" tone.

"It's a little more complicated than that." Chloe sighed. She wasn't sure how much she was going to tell them, but she wasn't ready to say anything quite yet. *Maybe on the bridge. That would be the right place.*

When they got off, they slipped past the crowds of large, slow-moving people who were taking pictures and standing around in aimless groups like the Golden Gate buffalo. Paul stopped at a machine to get a bottle of Coke. Once upon a time he would have finished it when they made it to the middle, and the three friends would have written a note and sealed it inside, tossing it into the water below. When they were even younger, they'd pretended that they were on an isolated little island and the bridge led to another world and it was the beginning of a long journey and quest for the three of them, together.

But now they tried to look as normal and unthreatening as possible to the action-figure National Guard. The days of throwing harmless things off the bridge were long, long over.

"It's like we live under martial law," Amy muttered.

"Uh, I think they're here to protect *us*," Paul protested.

"I like your skirt," Chloe said, noticing the segmented and flaring jean mini Amy sported, almost like a loose tutu.

"Thanks," Amy said shyly. "I made it last week. I'm thinking about doing a whole matching set, like 'Jeans Princess.'" She pointed her foot and revealed, under the silver puffy coat, matching jean leg warmers, kind of like bell-bottoms without the rest of the pants attached. Chloe wasn't sure *she* would wear them, but it was definitely a cool idea.

"Your mom should totally let you work at Pateena's."

"*Tell* me about it," Amy said, kicking a rock. She kicked it again with her other foot and then really got into it, kicking it back and forth like a soccer ball before accidentally shooting it twenty feet or so ahead. She ran after it, puffy coat flying. Chloe laughed.

"Tuesday was our anniversary," Paul said.

"Yeah?"

"She made me a card. And wrote me a poem," he

231

added cryptically, no expression on his face. Chloe studied him for a moment before smiling.

"At least she didn't perform it in front of a crowd," she pointed out.

"Yeah," was all he said, with a heavily relieved sigh.

They caught up to Amy at the midpoint. She was already leaning over, spitting.

"I've told you that's a *myth*," Paul said, putting his hands on his hips in exasperation.

"No, it's not," Chloe argued, leaning over and spitting herself. "If you get it just right with the wind—it really *does* fly back up."

"You two are disgusting," he said, turning around with his back to the rail. He pulled a cigarette out of his pocket and cupped his hand against the wind to light it. Red sunlight lit his face from below as if he was in front of a fire.

Unfortunately, when the wind blew the other way, the smoke completely overpowered her newly heightened sense of smell. She turned her head into the wind, trying not to gag.

"You gonna jump off *this* rail?" Amy asked, jerking her thumb at it.

Chloe smiled. "No, I don't think so. The boys in green over there wouldn't like it too much."

"Hey, I got it!" Paul suddenly said, holding his arms out like he was literally hit by an idea. "You're *supposed* to be dead! From the fall. And now, like in those Final Destination movies, death is doing everything it can to reclaim you! That *totally* explains the homeless guy and that guy who tried to kill you."

"Um, *thanks* for that heartening interpretation," Chloe said, "but if that were true, it wouldn't just be people after me—random things, like cars and—well, this *bridge* would collapse and try to do me in."

"Oh. Yeah." Paul took a step or two backward, looking at the ground.

"Anyway, like I said, it's a little more complicated than that."

"What were you *doing* walking by yourself at night, anyway? *Twice?*" Amy demanded, kicking the little rock between her feet and moving on across to the other side.

The three continued moseying along the bridge, long black shadows behind them. There were a few other people enjoying the sunset, and occasionally a cyclist would go whizzing by. Ahead of them the bridge was empty; they had it all to themselves, like the end of a movie. This was it. This was the moment. Here was where she decided how much to tell them.

Chloe took a deep breath.

A figure stepped out in front of them from the car side, blocking their path.

"Um, guys, you the know the weirdo with the blades—*not* the bum?"

"Yeah?" Paul and Amy asked; they were holding hands.

"That's him." She pointed.

The Rogue stood his ground and smiled.

Twenty

"Chloe King."

He held a dagger in each hand and wore no jacket tonight, just a black turtleneck that looked it was made of neoprene—or was hiding armor underneath. *Just the sort of thing Brian would wear,* Chloe noted distractedly. The pants and boots were the same as the other night; she could see his thick blond hair held back in a ponytail that just ended at the bottom of his neck.

"Hey," Paul yelled, thinking fast. "HEY!" he yelled, cupping his hands in the direction of the National Guard. But his words died in the wind.

"You think your human friends are going to help save you?" the man asked with feigned surprise. "Just because you keep company with them doesn't mean you're one of them."

"Ho-ly shit," Amy said, openmouthed.

"Um, *yeah* . . ." Chloe estimated the distance between

them—about twenty-five feet. Good enough for a head start? *What about Paul and Amy?*

"I have no idea what you're talking about," Chloe shouted back.

"They don't know your *true nature*?" the man asked, eyes widening.

"Do we all run in different directions?" Amy whispered, beginning to get really scared. "Or what?"

"They *should*." He walked forward slowly, looking Amy and Paul each in the eye, back and forth, like a cobra deciding where to strike first. "She's not really your friend. She isn't even your kind. *Our* kind," the man said, desperate to make them understand. "Her people want nothing less than the complete destruction of humanity. To rule the world. To defy God Himself."

"Chloe . . . ?" Paul asked. He wasn't referring to the killer's speech; like Amy, he was wondering what they should do. Without thinking or talking about it, the three of them began to back away slowly, at the same pace at which the man advanced.

"Run," Chloe hissed. "Run *now*!"

Paul and Amy ran.

The Rogue laughed, turning to watch her friends go. "How sweet—are you protecting them? Or protecting the truth about yourself!"

Chloe sensed this was it. And she was right: by the time he looked back and threw his daggers, she had already dropped to all fours and leapt at him. She heard the blades whoosh with deadly accuracy over her head; they would have been firmly buried in her stomach had she remained standing.

Two handsprings later she launched herself with a roar at his chest, not really thinking out her attack, just using momentum, movement, and surprise to gain the upper hand, if only for a second.

Just before her claws managed to sink into his flesh, he reached below her, grabbing and pushing, using her own weight to throw her over his head past him. She landed on the ground safely, not with a tuck and roll, but on all fours.

Flying daggers don't kill people, Chloe thought, leaping sidewise at the last minute to avoid one, grabbing the pedestrian rail. *People kill people.*

"It doesn't matter," he shouted. "Even if you are the One, I have blades enough for all of you."

What the hell does that mean? And more to the point, why doesn't he carry a gun like a normal psychopath? Chloe swung around so she was standing on the rail and lightly ran along it until she came to a slender blue lamppost. She leapt and clung to the sides, shimmying up it. A loud clank indicated a blade that must have just missed one of her feet, hitting the pole instead.

Chloe leapt to the next support without thinking, crossing ten feet of air right over his head. Shuriken whistled up into the sky behind her. She turned as if to leap back again, as if she were confused and frightened and not thinking.

At the last minute she dove right for him.

Finally her claws made contact with his flesh, skimming over some of the Kevlar or whatever he wore, sinking in where it ended. They struggled closely for a moment, landing together on the ground with a bone-jarring thud. Chloe concentrated on just digging in wherever her claws could reach and keeping her legs moving, hopefully doing some damage near his crotch. He tried to lock his own legs around her; they were very strong, almost stony with muscle. Just before her strength gave out, Chloe leapt away again. As soon as she was up, she turned around to face him, ready for his next attack.

There was a deadly whir that just skimmed her ears, followed by a clang of metal on metal. A throwing star shot by her head and bounced off the stanchion just above the Rogue, who was already getting up. Chloe spun around.

Standing on the other side of the Rogue, about twenty feet away, was Brian. He had a pained look on his face and another throwing star in his hand.

Brian . . . ? Chloe had a hard time processing what she was seeing, but there was no mistaking the weapon he held.

Pain and despair and rage beat down on her. She knew she should concentrate on the fact that she had *two* attackers now, but Chloe was suddenly exhausted by this unexpected betrayal. So much made sense now. . . . The note came back to her: *Be wary of the company you keep.*

He started walking toward her.

"Get *away* from me, you—*freak!*" Chloe screamed. "You *were* stalking me. I can't believe how real it seemed. . . . Nothing we did meant . . . anything!"

"Chloe, no! I . . ."

There was a scraping noise behind her. Chloe panicked and spun around. Her assassin was already up and advancing on her. He saw Brian and smiled.

She was trapped in between them.

Chloe looked around wildly; her only escape was off the bridge. She started toward the rail.

"No!" Brian shouted. "Chloe!"

But someone leapt at Brian, arms wide and claws extended. Chloe got a glimpse of furious ice blue eyes and a shock of honey hair before the two tumbled into an angry, kicking struggle on the ground.

Alyec. Alyec was the other cat person. She had misread *all* of the clues about both of them. Somehow she should have known. . . .

"I've got him," Alyec yelled. "Get that motherfucker . . . !"

Chloe felt new strength within her. *This* was her partner; he had her back. Now it was up to her. She turned to face the Rogue.

His turtleneck was torn to shreds on the right half of his body; black tatters and blood flowed down his skin. There was a strange tattoo on his arm, but she couldn't quite make it out. Blood dripped from the corner of his mouth, probably from his head hitting the ground. He wiped at it and spat out more.

She waited for him to say something profound, like in the movies, but instead he suddenly began throwing what seemed like dozens of throwing stars at her that appeared at his fingertips like roses from a magician's.

She danced and leapt and did handsprings and managed to avoid most of the shuriken.

"Another of my Order has come to watch and help with the cause!" He threw them harder and harder.

Chloe twisted and fell as a throwing star buried itself in her side.

"You thought he was your what—boyfriend? He was hunting you, just like I was." He laughed.

As Chloe struggled to get up, he reached down to the side of his pants and pulled out something that was smaller than a machete but larger than his previous blades. The pain in her side was like fire; every time she moved, it felt like her body was ripping apart.

He began advancing on her.

The wind whistled in Chloe's hair. She watched him come at her slowly, pain masking sound and thought. She could vaguely hear Brian and Alyec shouting obscenities at each other and the occasional muffled thump as one of them landed a blow.

There really *was* a very good chance that if no one helped her, she was going to die.

And then something inside her snapped.

How dare you?

"How *dare* you!" she screamed. Chloe ripped the shuriken out of her side and threw it to the ground, wincing at the pain. "What the *hell* did I ever do to *you*? Or *anyone*? I didn't ask for *any* of this!"

And she ran at him, blind rage eclipsing the pain.

He swung his blade down, but she lunged to the side and swiped her hand against his arm, raking her claws down it. He cried out, forced to switch the knife to his left hand. Chloe hadn't finished moving, though. She spun and kicked him on the back of his neck with her toes, smashing the Kevlar collar into his flesh.

"Fuck you," she screamed. "Get out of my *life*!"

The hot, blind rage was cooling, replaced with something much more cold and logical. She saw clearly ahead of time every punch, kick, and swipe—and followed up with an immediate counterattack. She never gave him time to draw another blade.

He backed up slowly until he was up against the rail. "How—many—others—have—you—killed?" With each word, she sent another kick into his stomach.

At the last minute he managed to launch himself so he was over the rail, keeping it between them.

"You fucking psycho," Chloe spat into his face.

Battered and bloody, he still managed a smile. "I do service for the Lord. His will be done."

"Yeah, well, tell that to the—"

And then he slipped.

241

Chloe was thrown off for a moment; this was something she hadn't expected.

"Chloe! Don't kill him!" Brian yelled. He tried to run over to stop her, but Alyec pulled him down to the ground again.

She leaned over, watching her assassin sway in the winds, struggling to hang on.

Finish him! Every part of her wanted to step on his fingers, to claw his face, to watch and smile as he slowly lost strength, slipped, and fell.

He tried to kill you! He hunted *you down, like you were prey!*

Even the human side of her agreed: this was a psycho who was better off *not* in the collective gene pool.

Then she offered him her hand.

I can't. Fighting is one thing—I can't kill someone in cold blood.

"You. On the bridge. Step away from the rail."

The electronically loud bullhorn noise made everyone spin. A helicopter rose up from below, aiming its spotlight along the bridge.

Chloe looked up as well—

And the Rogue fell.

Twenty-one

"No!" she cried, trying to grab after him. But there was only air.

"They're coming," Brian said, to no one in particular.

Chloe was still leaning over the rail, looking at the water in shock and disbelief. She doubted that he would come back the way she had from her own fall. It was like a book had suddenly closed and she would never be able to open it and read it again—find out why he was filled with hate. Instead of relief she felt a lack of closure, even a little loss.

"We've got to get out of here," Alyec said, grabbing Chloe's arm and pulling her away.

The two of them ran.

Although she was exhausted from the fight and felt some of her strength bleeding out of the wound in her side, Chloe still found a joy in running. When she leapt onto the handrail at the end to jump down off the bridge, tightrope running along its slick metal surface, Alyec was right behind her.

She chose to go up to the Marin Headlands; she leapt in between passing cars, up and over fences like she was flying. Alyec was beside her. He kept up with her, scrambling up the hill, jumping over rocks with an extremely familiar feline grace.

When she looked over at him, he grinned.

The other cat person.

A friend.

They crested the hill and started down the other side. The sky in the west was still its cartoon pink and orange; couples and families dotted the headlands watching it, cuddled in blankets and sipping from thermoses.

They had long outpaced the National Guard on foot, but the helicopter swept down the bridge and over the water, looking for trouble. The whole thing had Amy and Paul written all over it—still trying to save her after she'd made them go.

Chloe leapt. It didn't matter. The helicopter wouldn't be able to track her and Alyec. They were too fast. She felt like screaming with joy.

Alyec screamed instead—in pain—and went down on one knee, tumbling into the dirt.

Chloe stopped immediately and ran over to see him. He held his leg; a throwing star stuck out of it.

"Shit," he grunted, pulling it out and wincing.

"What the—?" Chloe turned around, looking for the attacker.

Brian stood twenty feet behind them, another star in his hand.

He began running toward them.

"That *bastard*!" Alyec growled, standing up with some difficulty.

Chloe put herself in front of him, between him and Brian. "Who is he? Why does he want to kill me?"

"He's a member of the Order of the Tenth Blade," Alyec spat. "I should have guessed before, the first time I saw him."

"Wait—Chloe—" Brian caught up to them. Chloe tensed, ready to spring.

"Coming to finish me off?" she demanded.

"I wasn't trying to *kill* you!" Brian protested. "I was trying to get *Alexander*!"

"Uh-huh," Chloe sneered. But . . . she really wanted to believe him. She wanted to believe that someone so close to her so quickly couldn't be capable of hunting her down and killing her. "And what about Alyec? Is he one of my 'race' that your . . . *friend* and you want to destroy?"

"I didn't mean to hurt you, but I had to stop you."

"Didn't mean to . . . ?" Alyec demanded, pointing at the blood running down his leg.

"I had to stop you," Brian reiterated. His brown eyes were wide, begging her to believe him. "If you keep heading down to the water . . . there are others, at least a dozen or more of . . . us, waiting for you, in case you do escape. Some with more . . . conventional weapons."

245

"Who the hell is the Tenth Blade?" Chloe demanded. "And what do you have to do with them?"

"Their only purpose is to kill people like us," Alyec said.

"Not all of you; that's not true. . . ."

"Tell that to the Rogue."

"Only the *dangerous* ones!"

"And what is Chloe? Dangerous?" Alyec growled and leapt at Brian, pushing past Chloe. His claws were fully extended; they were shorter and thicker than Chloe's. He was aiming for Brian's neck.

"STOP," Chloe said, pushing him out of the way and planting a firm hand on Alyec's shoulder to stop him. But he was angry, raging, out of control.

Without thinking, she took her hand and cuffed him on the side of the head to snap him out of it.

Like a cat cuffs her kittens, she realized after she did it.

Alyec shook his head, dazed, but stumbled back.

"Is that why you hung out with me?" Chloe demanded. "To keep tabs on me so they could kill me?" She looked Brian in the eye. So much made sense now—and it was a thousand times worse than she'd ever thought.

"No! I mean, I was supposed to keep track of you, learn about you, talk to you. Become . . . friends." They held each other's eyes for a moment; it was obvious he meant something else entirely. He hung his head. "Then I found out the Rogue was after you, and I wanted to stay by you and protect you—when I couldn't convince them to call him off."

"Don't believe him! Stupid monkey," Alyec said.

"I'm here talking to you, aren't I?" Brian shouted at him. "Why would I lie *now*?"

"I can't believe it." Chloe backed away from him. "I can't believe you're part of a group that wants me *dead*."

"It's more complicated than that, Chloe," Brian said tiredly. "Even Alyec can tell you that."

"Why did you warn me to stay away from him?" Chloe demanded. "Because you didn't want me learning the truth?"

"No. Alyec is a known . . . troublemaker. I didn't want you drawing attention to yourself, falling in with the wrong crowd."

"Looks like I fell in with the *right* crowd," Chloe said disgustedly. "Finally." She ducked down and put Alyec's arm around her shoulders to help him walk. "A couple of years of working out in the 'real world' so you could be a *zoology major*?"

Brian flushed with shame. "Chloe, I really liked—I really like you."

"Whatever," Chloe said, leading Alyec away.

Epilogue

Alyec lay on her couch, his injured leg raised. It wasn't that large a cut, but the shuriken had sliced through tendon, making it impossible for him to walk. Chloe's own wound on her side had stopped bleeding but continued to ache.

Dazed, exhausted from the fight, and unsure what else to do, Chloe took some taquitos from the freezer and put them in the microwave. She had maybe an hour before her mom came home and serious explanations began if Alyec wasn't gone.

"This sucks." Alyec swore, looking at the cut.

Leaning against the stove, Chloe put her hands to her face and finally began to cry.

"Hey, don't do that," Alyec said, pushing himself up and hobbling over to her. He put an arm around Chloe. "It's very confusing, I know. . . . But don't worry! Everything will be explained. There's so much you need to know—about who you are and where you came from. And you will be safe, I promise. There are these people you should meet now; I think you'll like them. . . ."

Chloe gave Alyec a small smile. Somehow she knew he didn't mean any of his friends from school. And that was fine by her.

As many as 1 in 3 Americans
who have HIV...don't know it.

TAKE CONTROL.
KNOW YOUR STATUS.
GET TESTED.

To learn more about HIV testing,
or get a free guide to HIV and
other sexually transmitted diseases:

www.knowhivaids.org
1-866-344-KNOW

Sign up for the CHECK YOUR PULSE
free teen e-mail book club!

 **FEATURING**

A new book discussion every month

Monthly book giveaways

Chapter excerpts

Book discussions with the authors

Literary horoscopes

Plus YOUR comments!

To sign up go to www.simonsays.com/simonpulse and
don't forget to CHECK YOUR PULSE!